SIPHON

A.A. MEDINA

"A.A. Medina is a talented writer. The pacing of this novella is mapped out with precision detail; not a single word wasted."

—Sadie Hartmann, *Scream Magazine*

"I had no idea what exactly to expect with this book but left knowing I'd read a pretty damn good novella."

—Grim Reader Reviews

"A.A. Medina's *Siphon* is a thoroughly enjoyable story of transformation and acceptance. At least that's how I interpreted it, and that's what I loved about this novella. It doesn't spoon feed you the facts, it leaves doors open."

—Kendall Reviews

"Well what can I say? WOW... This is a really great intense story...I was bearing witness to a descent into madness."

—Housewife of Horror

"The cadence of the story was beautifully choreographed and flowed like a well-orchestrated horror symphony. This was original, a bit peculiar, and out of the ordinary with a very strange and dark sense of humor thrown in to make it all the more eerie and fascinating."

—Book Review Village

To my amazing wife, Samantha, who knows when—and when not—to put up with my bullshit.

"UNFORTUNATELY THERE CAN BE NO DOUBT THAT MAN IS, ON THE WHOLE, LESS GOOD THAN HE IMAGINES HIMSELF OR WANTS TO BE. EVERYONE CARRIES A SHADOW, AND THE LESS IT IS EMBODIED IN THE INDIVIDUAL'S CONSCIOUS LIFE, THE BLACKER AND DENSER IT IS. AT ALL COUNTS, IT FORMS AN UNCONSCIOUS SNAG, THWARTING OUR MOST WELL-MEANT INTENTIONS."

— CARL JUNG

Neglected...

Starved...
The lack of sustenance is sustenance...

Shackles...
They twist and they strain.

Power.

No value.
No release.

Where is the catalyst?

Impetus.

Release.

Where?

When?

Primal.

Suppression.

Darkness.
A fissure. A rift.

Light oozes through the seam...

Catalyst...

What are you?

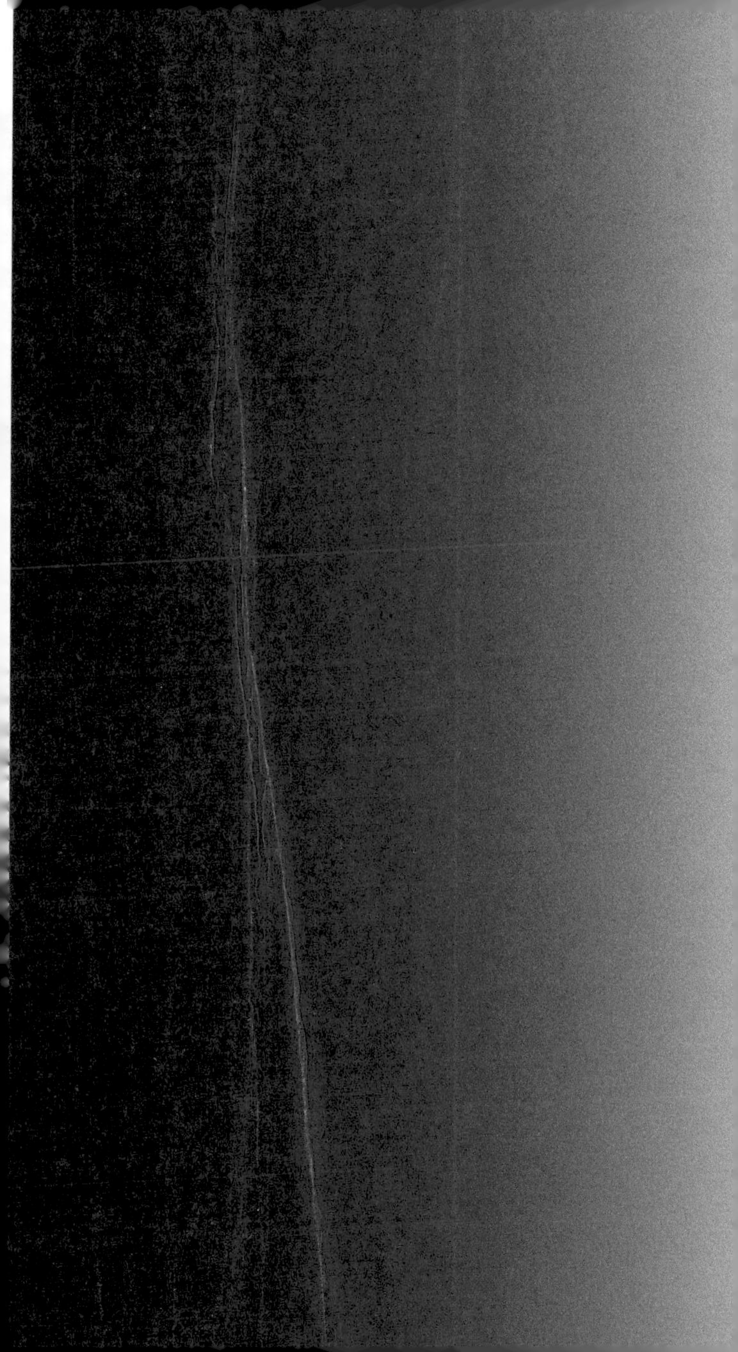

ONE

nother all-nighter?" A gentle voice ripped me from my sitting slumber.

Startled, I jolted my head up and wiped the drool that had concentrated on the mentolabial fold above my butt-chin. I had fallen asleep slumped over my desk again; my head nestled on my crossed arms and I didn't even bother to move the array of loose documents and manila folders out of the way. It didn't matter how much coffee I had dropped down my gullet, there was something about the sustained hum of a centrifuge at four in the morning that induced inescapable drowsiness.

Frantic, I patted the chest pocket of my button-up and side pockets of my lab coat. I upheaved the papers on my desk, but I couldn't find my glasses. I was incapable of identifying anything more than six inches in front of me. Wendy plucked the spectacles off the top of my balding head and waved them in front of me.

"Looking for these, silly?"

My face burned red with embarrassment. I rushed to diffuse the awkward silence.

"I'd lose my head if it weren't attached," I said. Dumb. What a cliché thing to say. Cleverness was never a quality of mine. Plus, my mind never functioned properly around Wendy, add the fact that I was still half asleep. I always felt like I was staring at her.

Wendy was young and blonde, maybe twenty-four or twenty-five. Whatever her age, I was easily ten years her elder. She held a manila folder jammed with documents and a vacutainer of blood against her chest with one hand while she fought a single lock of hair that always seemed to find its way from behind her ear with the other. Her eyes were big and green and reminded me of a murky pond on a sunny day.

"How was your night, Wendy?" I asked as I swiveled in my office chair to face her. I crossed my legs like a psychiatrist about to shrink her head.

"Hmm..." Wendy pondered. "Ya' know, the usual..."

I couldn't focus on her words. She'd slide

her bottom lip ever so slightly under her front teeth whenever she pondered—I lived for that. Sometimes I'd ask her puzzling questions only to watch her perform this provocative, but unintendedly so, act. It had been a few moments since Wendy had stopped talking. Her eyes wandered as she waited for a response. I had to force myself away from my lustrous gaze.

"Sorry," I said, "still a little out of it. Sounds like an amazing night to me." I had no idea what she said.

"Anyway," Wendy said, "Dr. Geraldo sent these in to get tested."

I checked my wristwatch and rubbed my cheek. It had been a few weeks since I've shaved. Catching my reflection in a refrigerator's glass door, it blended with the rows of blood-filled vacutainers within. At that moment, I resembled a skinny George Costanza, but with a little more hair, wider eyes, and if he were strung out on an array of narcotics.

"You could set those down on the counter." I pointed behind her to the countertop where the centrifuge and other medical machinery resided.

Wendy turned to place the sample in the refrigerator and cleared room to place the stack of documents she'd been holding.

I observed her body. The color of her scrubs were just a few shades darker pink than the color of her flesh. They were hemmed just right and hugged her curves, and easily provoked thoughts that were not safe for work. The material was thin and didn't leave much to the imagination. I wasn't ready to uncross my legs just yet.

"What's your ETA on these?" Wendy asked. "He said he needed them as soon as possible."

"Tell Dr. Geraldo it's going to have to wait until later."

I far exceeded my twelve-hour shift at Claybrook Medical Center. The hospital was centrally located in Claybrook City, a metropolis where a couple hundred-thousand faceless blobs commute to and from fuck knows or cares where. Business was booming at the hospital this time of year. There was something about the holiday season that brought the best out in people. However, this year was a little different—it had seemed like the number of homicides, attempted homicides, and suicides was up threefold from last year.

"I've been stuck here for..." I checked my watch again. "Almost fifteen hours. It's time for me to go home and get some rest. I'm due back later tonight."

"Well, what should I tell him?" She bit her lip and narrowed her brow.

Curse my overactive libido.

"Shift is up. I went home." I clawed around the mess on my desk for my car keys. When I looked up, I saw that Wendy was tense. "Hey," I said in my brightest voice, "but don't you worry. I'll be back soon. I just need a couple hours."

"He's not gonna be happy."

"He never is," I said.

Wendy smirked. At least we shared something in common. Then again, I don't think anyone had feelings other than disdain for Dr. Geraldo.

"Go get some sleep, Dr. Phillips," Wendy said. "I'll see you later."

"I told you, call me Gary." I wanted nothing more than to hear my name escape her supple, pink lips.

Wendy responded with a half-hearted smile instead. It was like she knew what I wanted but was being a tease.

I took off my lab coat and hung it on the hanger fastened to the back of the door. "Bye, Wendy."

My drive home from the hospital wasn't too

bad. Unlike most in the medical field, I didn't own a huge house in the suburbs or a sleek suite in the better part of the city. I didn't own a convertible or a hummer and leave it in my driveway for the entire world to see. I wasn't about conspicuous consumption or status symbols. It's all a bunch of bullshit.

However, if I were even financially capable of indulging, it wouldn't be with a plethora of luxury vehicles or a house with more rooms than I'd care to use. Rather, it would be the illustrious trophy wife. Blonde, smiling, classy... Young. Ready to cater to my every want or need or desire when I've returned from a long day's work. More often than not, I found myself daydreaming of taking the lucky lady to parties and social gatherings. I would even consider joining a country club just so I could flaunt her around.

A man can dream, can't he?

I was alone when I arrived at my small townhouse a few miles from the hospital. That meant it was going to be a good day. I was too young to remember my parents passing away, since then, my grandfather took care of me. However, over time, the roles reversed.

Planning on doing what I could only hope I

would be able to do most days when my grandfather wasn't home demanding every free second of my time, I made sure my thick, purple curtains were drawn closed. I didn't need any neighbors or the sun sneaking a peek at me losing my dignity for the day. Stripping off my clothes, I readied my smartphone and climbed into bed.

Wendy Leann Carter was her full name. Kids these days, they post all kinds of things on their various social media profiles—phone numbers, addresses, daily routines, and photos in bikinis and sexy dresses. The ritual had become all too familiar to me. I was obsessed. I knew she had a cluster of freckles above her left breast. I knew she was a dog lover. I knew she had a tattoo that read "Peace & Love" with a flower on her right hip about six inches below her belly button. It was a Yellow Germini or a Gerber Daisy, I wasn't too sure. I knew she liked beer pong, too much.

I knew more than I should.

My favorite photo was the seventh one in a collection she suitably named "Beach Time!!!" Wendy was making a peace sign with her fingers and biting her lower lip. She wore a white bikini; the water must've been cold that day. I saved that photo for last. That photo was for the final stretch.

The Big Finish.

Time stood still when I visited The Beach. My eyes darted from Wendy's face to her body then back to her face. The pressure grew and the lactic acid felt like it was eating away at my forearm. There was an urge to close my eyes, but a strange sense of guilt kept them locked on her pair of murky ponds. I curled my toes and relaxed my neck; a euphoric wave washed over my body. There was a sense of renewal with every release, but this time my grand crescendo was stifled when my bedroom door violently flung open.

TWO

An unanticipated return.

A shock.

An untimely release.

Soiled sheets evermore.

My left hand fumbled my phone and I was forced to flee The Beach. I pulled my duvet up to my bare chest just as the intruder stuck his head in the door.

"Gary!" The wrinkled head, pockmarked with liver-spots, growled. "What the fuck?"

"I'm trying to sleep, Grandpa," I shrilled, but my grandfather's bulldog face didn't seem to care.

I was not in the mood, let alone in the position to have a discussion with another living being—especially Sergeant Francis K. Phillips.

Naked and sullied under my sheets, my right palm sticky and moist as a held onto myself like an 'oh-shit' handle in an off-road vehicle. I was paralyzed while the distress crept through my veins. No one wants to see their grandpa's face as they climax.

"You were supposed 'ta pick me up from the casino, you little shit," Francis said. He favored his real leg as he leaned against my dusty dresser next to the doorway. He lost the other leg in the war, not from the war. Dirty needle. Vietnam ruined a whole generation of men.

"You were supposed to take the shuttle back," I squealed. I managed to release myself and subtly wipe my shame on the bed spread. "You're not even supposed to be back until tomorrow. I got you a hotel room."

Francis' head bobbled and he belched something vile. The stench cloud of whisky, fried shrimp, and bile was almost visible.

"How much did you lose?" I asked.

"Doesn't matter," Francis said. His glossy eyes avoided any contact with mine. He was drunk, like always.

At that moment, I found some solace in that maybe he didn't realize what he walked in on.

"Doesn't matter?" I repeated.

"Doesn't. Fuckin'. Matter."

"All of it?" I asked. "All that I gave you?"

Francis snatched one of my many novels stacked on top of the dresser next to him and flung it at me. It missed but knocked over the assortment of empty beer cans and water bottles stacked on my nightstand that I've been meaning to throw away.

"Get off 're ass and go to the store," Francis said. "There's no beer in the fridge."

"I'll bring some home after work. I need to get some slee— "

"Now!" Francis threw another book. This time, it pelted my ribs. "And clean 're fuckin' room. It's disgusting." Francis turned and hobbled down the hall.

I waited for a moment with the hope that he would pass out. Maybe I could get a few decent hours of sleep.

"Now!" Francis shouted. His voice bounced through the hallway.

It was about a mile to the nearest liquor store. I decided to walk. It would give my grandfather enough time to fall dead asleep, or just dead, by the time I returned. Don't get me wrong, I loved my grandfather. At least I thought I had to. Francis was the only family I had, and I didn't know anyone else close enough to call them friends. My parents died when I was a toddler; I have no recollection of them. Just a shoebox of photos and a copy of my mother's unfinished manuscript.

Claybrook City was a shithole, but the area I lived in wasn't too bad, for the most part. There was the chance of running into the occasional tweeker or junkie. No one said 'hi' as they passed, not even a nod of the head. At least not to me. Everyone had something to do, somewhere to go, and no time to acknowledge their shared existence. The drab gray concrete walls of the buildings downtown matched the seemingly year-round drab gray clouds that blanketed the city.

Meandering down the filthy sidewalk, I periodically stopped to observe the products displayed through the shop's windows. Pale, flower-patterned dresses, scarves, and gaudy brimmed hats. Cafes and second-hand stores. A hipster's consumer paradise. That wasn't the kind of stuff I was into, but I didn't mind it either. The pedestrians were young and full of life, and I walked among them, unnoticed.

I entered the liquor store and grabbed a twelve pack of cat piss flavored water. Francis was more of a quantity-over-quality kind of guy. Pretending to peruse the aisles, I waited for the girl at the counter to get off the phone. She argued with someone, probably her boyfriend. I didn't want to interrupt, but I only had so long to try and get some sleep.

"No, I did not fuck Raul," she hissed into her phone. Her eyes rose to meet mine; I didn't realize I was staring. "I have to go. I'm at work." She slammed her phone on the counter. "Can I help you?"

"I'm ready to check out," I said. "A pack of Lucky Strikes, too. No filter, please." The girl took her time retrieving the smokes from the back wall. I checked my wristwatch; it was twenty passed six. "Fuck me," I muttered under my breath.

"Excuse me?" She heard me.

"No, no," I stumbled over my words, "not you. It's just getting late is all." I was due back at the hospital in just over three hours.

I paid the girl, whom I was convinced was high as a kite on something, and didn't take my time meandering back home.

Please be asleep.

Please be asleep.

Please be asleep.

Please be dead, I thought to myself as I opened the front door.

"What the fuck took you so long?"

I hadn't got a foot in the door. I didn't bother to answer. Francis sat in his moldy recliner watching football. I walked past him and into the small galley kitchen, placed the cat piss in the fridge and the smokes on the counter. Retrieving a bottle of valium I kept in the cupboard above the fridge, I plucked four—two for me, two for grandpa—from the bottle and placed it back in the cupboard. I ground up the two for Francis in a generic, plastic pill-grinder complete with crank. They sold them at most pharmacies for about ten bucks. I snatched a beer from the fridge, opened it, and funneled the freshly ground valium powder in it. I grabbed a beer for myself and used it to chase my dosage. I swirled contaminated beer around until the powder was nice and dissolved. This would give me a few hours of peace, I figured.

"Here," I said. "Now, please don't bother me. I need to get some sleep before I head back to work." I tossed the Lucky Strikes on Francis' lap and placed the special beer on the old, splintered oak end-table next to him. He responded with a grunt and a shoo of his hand.

I returned to my room, anxious to lay down before the valium kicked in.

I laid there and watched the ceiling fan. It was on high. It spun too fast. It creaked in the rhythm of a beating heart. The air reeked of stale cigarettes and dust being perpetually cycled and recycled through the room. I wanted to open the window, but I couldn't bring myself to get out of bed. I thought about revisiting The Beach, this time I was sure I wouldn't be interrupted, but I was too tired. I fought the urge to check the time because if I knew exactly how much time I lacked, it would only leave me more restless. So, I just laid there. Too tired.

I turned on the television mounted on the wall across the foot of my bed. Some lucky asshole won the lottery that day and some not-so-lucky asshole was shot dead at the shopping mall a few miles down the street. They shared equal airtime on every news program.

Eventually, I came across a made-for-television vampire drama. The scene: A half-naked woman laid in bed and pretended to be asleep. A handsome, pale fella floated through her open window. As he approached, he revealed his fangs. Suddenly, she pulled a cross from under her sheets, presented it to him, and he took off, hissing and snarling back into the night.

The room became cold and my fingers went numb. In the movie, as the defiant bimbo made her way into the castle to drive the stake through the poor, misunderstood vampire's heart, I started to drift.

My body was heavy, but I still felt alert. I wasn't sure if my eyes were closed, but it was the closest thing to sleeping in a bed I've had in a long while. My heart synced up with the ceiling fan, my mind mesmerized by its gyration and everything else faded away. I laid there.

Time had ceased to exist.

My cellphone rattled on the Ikea nightstand. Without looking, I flung my hand to the side and plucked it from its charger. Eight missed calls from Dr. Geraldo.

Time sure as hell still existed.

"Shit."

THREE

I don't remember the drive back to the hospital. I was surprised I didn't kill myself or anyone else. At night, downtown became a bar crawl. It was difficult enough to navigate through the cesspool of dumb, drunk collection of meatheads, hipsters, and sluts while sober.

In the blindingly bright, white hallway, I was confronted by Dr. Lucas Geraldo. The youngest member on the Board of Trustees. On average, in the case of hospitals, people usually don't rise to that position until they are over fifty. Nationwide, it is extremely rare to have a Trustee younger than fifty, but Dr. Geraldo was a twenty-eight-year-old. Overachiever. Shithead. The Golden Boy. The son of someone powerful and important. He strolled up and down the halls like an S.S. Overseer.

"Dr. Phillips," Little Hitler barked, "I've been

trying to contact you for over an hour now. What seems to be your malfunction?"

"No malfunction, Sir," I said. "I was running late and got stuck in— "

"You know how I feel about excuses."

"Yes, I do, Dr. Geraldo." My fingernails dug into my palms. "It won't happen again."

"Let's hope not," Satan said. "I'm still waiting on the results for..." He flipped through the sheets on his clipboard, "Rebecca Turner. I needed those done this morning."

"Who?" I regrettably asked.

"I had Ms. Carter bring you the samples this morning." His tone was more than condescending.

"Oh, yes." I wanted to punch him in the Adam's Apple. I wanted to rip out his jugular and smack him upside the head with it. I fantasized about snatching his thin, wire glasses off his face and shoving them down his stupid throat and watching him choke while I cupped my ear and listened to the air struggling to bypass his bifocals while he pleaded for mercy. Then I'd laugh manically in his young, chiseled face.

"I'll get right on that, Sir." I started to walk past him, but he side-stepped in front of me.

"One more thing, Dr. Phillips," Dr. Geraldo

said. "It wouldn't hurt to shave and comb your hair. Clean up a little. This isn't an urgent care in the slums. We're professionals here."

Before I could respond, Dr. Geraldo strutted away. His eyes were already locked onto another resident as he continued his micromanagement campaign.

I entered the lab, threw on my lab coat, and sat down at my desk. The stack of manila folders plopped down on my ever-growing mess doubled during the hours I was gone. Glancing at the fridge full of vacutainers, they doubled as well. I caught my reflection. I looked almost dead.

Rebecca... Rebecca...

I couldn't remember the last name, but I had to get her analysis done first. The last thing I wanted was Dr. Geraldo further up my ass.

Turner!

I searched the stack of documents, but it wasn't there. I scoured the top of my desk and every drawer. It was nowhere to be found. Then I remembered I told Wendy to place it on the counter.

Fortunately, no one was there to witness my miniature nervous breakdown. The valium still flowed through my body. Even the simplest physical or cognitive tasks proved to be straining. I retrieved the bottle of Adderall from the back of my desk drawer, popped a few in my mouth, and chased it with a Styrofoam cup of cold coffee from the night before.

Time to get to work.

Rebecca Turner's profile called for an M.C.V. or mean corpuscular volume. It was a measure of the average red blood cells. It was a way to test for anemia, whether microcytic anemia if the M.C.V. was lower than normal, or a macrocytic anemia if it was higher. The test was completely automated; all I had to do was throw the sample into the centrifuge which compacted the erythrocytes. The vacutainer labeled "Turner, Rebecca" was in the refrigerator right where Wendy left it.

It was a haze, but the routine was so repetitive that I felt more robot than human. Folder after folder, vacutainer after vacutainer, blood, blood, and more blood, and just when I started to make a dent in my never-ending queue of labor, a faceless nurse, phlebotomist, or fifth-dimensional being, as far as I knew, dropped off another load. The life of a hematopathologist.

Most tests were preliminary when ran at the hospital. Most of them came up normal or nothing too out of the ordinary, but not today. Two in a row tested positive for H.I.V., some cancers, a handful of H.P.V. positives, and a bunch of news-to-them diabetics.

I was exhausted. It was about the time I would usually lay my head in my arms and close my eyes to kill a few hours. The centrifuge hummed and I turned off half of the overhead lights. It gave the room a warm, soft, luminescent glow. Instead, I hustled.

When handling sensitive material—blood in glass tubes and crucial information about the livelihood of people I'd never meet—I knew I had to work slow, careful, with grace, without shaky hands, with a keen eye and a sharp mind. So, there I am, excessive fatigue and under the influence of downers. And jittery from the uppers.

Amid retrieving multiple vacutainers from the refrigerator, I dropped one. It shattered, and chilled blood oozed onto the dirty linoleum floor.

Cursing through my clenched jaw, I squeezed the bridge of my nose and accessed the damage. I slid the other two vacutainers I was holding into my lab coat pocket and reached for the paper towels. Quilted. I knelt to clean it up, but then something happened.

I leered at the human oil crawl toward me. In that moment, my mind was empty. Not a loss-for-words empty or nodding-off empty. But, *empty*. No worries, no feelings, no opinions, no identity. No longer was I tired, but I was not awake either.

A comfortable void.

Nothing mattered. Not I or anyone else. I wasn't sure how long I must've been on my knees as I gazed at the pool of vital, room-temperature fluid. My mind was a dark abyss, my body was a barren cavity. I've heard of out-of-body experiences before, but I'd never experienced one myself. I, or—for lack of a better word—my soul, watched as my body was taken hostage by another being. A stronger being. A godly being. And then it pulled me back in with it.

The stillness was broken and the vacuum was filled as I jolted back into my body, yet I was still unable to move. My eyes forced to fixate on the blood that had started to congeal. At first, the voice was just a whisper. It was confident, omnipresent, and not long after it felt like a loudspeaker was installed inside my skull. A mantra, it repeated:
There is an urge inside you...
... which cannot be satisfied...
... with conventional methods.

My hand extended in front of my body and reached for the blood. My arms were shaking. I couldn't help but think that the puppet master who'd hijacked my body was a bit nervous. I didn't fight it, though. Even if I wanted to, I wouldn't know how.

My index finger swiped the floor and collected the coagulated mess as casually as one would dip a stick of celery into a jar of peanut butter. Just the touch was orgasmic. I wanted it inside me. I couldn't imagine living without it inside me.

There is an urge inside you...

Like a puppy anxiously awaiting table scraps from their master, I longed for my bloody finger to find my mouth.

"Come on, come on," I heard myself whisper, "almost there." That's when my hand stopped. Only a few inches from my lips like a carrot on a stick. "Come on!" my voice boomed from deep within my gut.

"Dr. Phillips," A soft voice uttered behind me. "Are you okay?"

As quickly as I lost control, I got it back. I pulled my hand away from my face and peered over my shoulder. Wendy had a single eyebrow raised and her lips were pursed.

"Ye— " I cleared my throat, "Yes, I'm alright. Just fumbled some samples." Sick to my stomach, I felt lost.

Wendy's eyes grew as she spotted the blood on my finger. "Oh, my god, did you cut yourself?"

"No, no," I choked on the words. "It's from the sample. I was just, I was just cleaning it up."

I struggled to my feet and sauntered to the sink. I ran the water but was reluctant to rinse the blood from my hand that had started to dry and emboss the maze of fingerprint on my index. I didn't crave it anymore, but I felt guilty. The guilt one feels after throwing away a full plate of food. What a waste.

Wendy set down her cardigan she had draped over her forearm and retrieved a fresh roll of paper towels from a supply drawer across the lab; I'm not sure where the ones I had went. She proceeded to get on her knees and clean up the mess.

"What happened?" Wendy said as she peeled shards of Pyrex from the crimson stain.

"Just a goof," I responded. There was an urge to confess my strange experience, but I didn't even know what had happened. "I lost control."

"Lost control?" Wendy cocked her head over her shoulder.

"Lost control of the vacutainer," I recovered. "I lost control of the vacutainer," I raised my voice over the running water. "Slipped out of my hand."

"Oh." Wendy returned her focus to the mess.

My ribs were a vice grip. My chest was caving in. A burning sensation crept up my throat and secretions of sour saliva coated my tongue. Like a geyser, vomit projected from my gaping mouth into the sink. An involuntary sticky, wet belch accompanied the flow of bile and regurgitated coffee.

"Dr. Phillips?" Wendy stood and caught sight of the vile particles that had splashed up and oozed off the sides of the stainless-steel sink. "Jesus— " Wendy dug her face into the crease of her elbow and gagged.

My lab coat was covered in greenish-brown vomit. It ran down my face and hung on my wiry, unshaved chin. I was absolutely horrified.

"I have to go," I said to myself. I snatched a handful of paper towels from the dispenser on the wall and vigorously wiped the spew from my face before turning to Wendy, "I have to go."

Wendy's eyes met mine, the bottom half of

her face still nestled in the pit of her elbow. She nodded her head.

"Just..." My eyes bounced around the room. It hurt to retain eye contact with her. "Just grab a custodian to clean it up."

Wendy continued to nod.

"I'm sorry, Wendy," I said. "I'm not feeling very well."

"I can see that," her voice muffled through the flesh of her arm. "Don't be sorry. It happens."

I didn't even finish cleaning my face before I headed for the door,

"Gary..."

"Yes?" My hand gripped the handle. I wanted nothing more than to get the fuck out of there.

"I know Dr. Geraldo is already hounding you," Wendy said, "what should I tell him? Just that you're sick?

"Tell him to go fuck himself."

I came to in my car. The engine was running, the radio was off, and the sun had already set. I knew I left the hospital around noon, so it had to be hours since then. I sat idle in my driveway and stared out at the front door of my townhouse. The vomit on my lab coat had dried into a flakey crust and it smelled like a shit myself.

Because I did.

Releasing my grip from the steering wheel, my fingers popped and cracked, and the flesh on my palms were red and blistered. I must have been white-knuckling it for hours. I thought about the drive home but came up blank. I popped open the door and peeled myself from the driver's seat. My legs were numb. I used the hood of my dinged-up hybrid as support as I wobbled my way to the pair of steps at the foot of my front door and caught myself on the doorknob before I fell to my knees on the concrete below. I twisted the doorknob and pushed it open. The momentum of the action left me propped up on my hands and knees, my arms shook, my shoulders burned.

I crawled into my living room and horse-kicked the front door closed behind me. Francis was asleep on his recliner, and I couldn't be more thankful for that. If he were to have seen me on all fours, covered in puke and soiled, I would have never heard the end of it.

The climb upstairs may as well have been equivalent to ascending Everest. My knees were scraped and bruised, my palms slick with pus, blood, and sweat, making it difficult to support myself on the hardwood stairs. My head pounded, my gut twisted, and I swore my eyes came closer to bulging out of their respective sockets with each stair conquered. That's the last thing I remembered before I woke up to Francis banging at the bathroom door.

I was nude, lying in the shower for God knows how long. His barrage of curses muffled by the water that clobbered my forehead. I sat up and turned off the shower.

What the fuck is happening?

"What in the fuckin' hell are you doin', boy?" Francis shouted. He vigorously jiggled the door handle. At least the unconscious me had the foresight to lock the door.

"Hold on," I said. Realizing my voice was but a whisper, I repeated myself, "Hold on."

It took a few minutes, but I pulled myself to my feet. The flesh around the lacerations on my knees were soft and curled. My fingers had pruned and the few unbusted blisters on my palms had become mushy sacs of goo. I opened the shower curtain and wrapped a towel around my waist.

"I was taking a shower," I said as I opened the door.

"For three hours?"

"Three hours?"

"The fuckin' water has been runnin' for three fuckin' hours, Gary," Francis said. "For fuck's sake, how many times can one man beat 'is meat?"

"I must've fallen asleep."

Francis sniffed the steam escaping the bathroom and pursed his lips tight. My slacks were inside-out on the floor between our feet. Francis lowered his head to examine them. "Is that shit?"

I was at a loss for words.

We just stood there fixated on what looked like a melted brownie infused with hues of forest green cemented to the ass-end of my inverted briefs. I'm sure Francis wanted to say something, but what could he? I didn't want to give him any more time to come up with something.

"I'm not feeling very well today, Grandpa."

Francis said nothing. He stared at me. I couldn't tell if it was a look of disgust, disappointment, or worry. Maybe it was a mixture of all three. He did us both a favor, turned, and retreated downstairs without a comment.

Control is something I've never had.

I didn't choose my profession—Francis did. He said the only men he respected were men with titles, and his grandson sure as hell had to have one. I had the choice of military or medical school. For eighteen-year-old, scrawny, scared, and awkward Gary, it was an easy decision.

I didn't choose where I lived—Francis did. My parents owned a quaint little house on about fifty acres of land about an hour outside of Claybrook City.

Being the next of kin, I owned the house. Francis hated that house and refused to live there. I rent out this shitty townhouse, in shitty downtown, to take care of his shitty ass... Well, figuratively shitty.

I examined the bathroom. My clothes were scattered across the floor. Feces, blood, and vomit smeared along the scuffed tile and dusty baseboards. Shower-water, and what smelled like piss, pooled up at the foot of the tub and around the base of the toilet.

I can't even control myself.

FOUR

I decided to take a few days sick leave. Dr. Geraldo wasn't happy, but he never was.

The last couple days, I went in and out of consciousness, but thankfully I always came to in my home. I'm not sure what I was doing while I was gone, but I never moved far from where I last remembered myself being. I didn't eat. The thought of food made my stomach somersault, yet my insides felt cavernous. Hollow.

I force fed myself a can of tuna with some saltines. Bad choice. No more than a few minutes after I scraped the tin can clean, I found myself heaving over the overflowing garbage bin tucked in the corner of the kitchen. Even water put up a fight; two out of every three sips refused to stay put when I swallowed.

I was so tired, but I couldn't sleep. When I laid down, all I could think about was how hungry

I was. When I ate, my body refused the contents. I must be withdrawing. The valiums were supposed to be an every-now-and-then occurrence. I guess I let that get away from me, over the last few weeks I'd become a habitual user. Out of the bottle of fifty, I had four left. The proof is in the proverbial pudding. The other medications, the drinking, that was a whole other thing.

If I wasn't going to sleep and I wasn't going to eat, then I figured I should be productive. I spent the greater part of the day picking up the rolling hills of garbage and dirty laundry that was on my bedroom floor. If time and energy allowed, I'd make a dent in my more pressing custodial duties. The bathroom remained in a desecrated state since that strange day. My soiled pants and vomit-covered lab coat were still festering on the piss-coated floor. I'd have to address that eventually, but for the time being I was using the downstairs' powder room.

While I organized my closet, I came across the large shoebox under another heap of laundry. The box was full of photos of my parents, my father's Claybrook City Police Department Badge, the keys to the house I inherited from them, and a few pieces of my mother's jewelry along with a copy of her unfinished manuscript; however, the box may as well have been empty, the relics meant nothing to me.

I have no recollection of my parents. They died, in what Francis told me, was a horrific car crash when I was a toddler. This box was full of things from a time that no longer mattered. Sure, if they were still alive, I wouldn't be stuck with Francis, but I can't say for sure if I'd be better off, or worse. I'm not the one to speculate what could have been.

After a quick flip through the photos and observation of my dad's badge, I pulled out my mother's manuscript. It had been over two decades since I last looked at it, so I decided to skim through and have one of those moments where you revisit something as an older, wiser adult and aim to catch the tiny details and nuances that flew over your head years ago.

Cynthia Campbell Phillips was my mother's name, or C. C. Phillips as it appeared on the cover page of the document. The working title of the manuscript was "Idée Fixe Foncé." French for "Fixed Idea Darkens" or something like that. It was a story about a woman named Victoria Bellevue. She had this unyielding desire to seduce the priest from the town church. At night, she would visit him at his home or at the church—wherever he was, she ended up—and tempt him with revealing attire. And when he slammed the door in her face and locked it, she would press her body against it and moan, describing all the dirty ways she would get him off.

Father Antonio, the priest, would come to her in her dreams and stimulate her in every way; manually, orally, traditionally, and unconventionally. He would act out her every fantasy and just before it all paid off, she would wake up in a horny flurry. Utterly unsatisfied. It drove her insane and she needed to get him to finish in the real world what he started in her dreams. It became such an obsession that she performed a ritual asking demonic forces for help.

Around five chapters in, right when it started to get good, the text trailed off into a nonsensible mashing of words for the next hundred or so pages. I remembered why I hadn't picked up the thing in so long. I set the stack of aging paper on top of my dresser with the rest of the books I had stacked there. Maybe one day I can pick up where she trailed off and finish her novel. Or maybe not. It was a romantic idea.

I must've drifted out of consciousness again. This time, however, when I came to, I was in the same exact position I was in when I left, sitting at the foot of my dresser. I thought I may have been sleeping, but that hope was squashed when I noticed the books I had stacked on top of it were knocked onto the floor. The pages of my mother's manuscript were somehow unbound and strewn across the room.

Fuck this.

With reluctance and dread, I decided to move on and clean the bathroom.

The stench was pungent. That was putting it lightly. The washer and dryer were downstairs, past the living room, and through the door on the left, right before the kitchen, and in the small one-car garage Francis used to store all his shit. I shoved my tainted clothes into a black garbage bag and tip-toed downstairs. Francis snored in his recliner, so I continued to sneak behind him and into the garage. The last thing I wanted was to wake Francis with a sack full of my most recent stigma like shit-stained clothes peddling Santa Claus.

I pulled out the crunchy socks from the bag

and tossed them in the top-loader. Next my crusty briefs, slacks, and button-up. The articles of clothing had all taken on a grime, a film, a texture that reminded me of day-old olive oil that'd one would find splattered on a stovetop. It even had the same color. I gagged and would have vomited if there were anything in my stomach to expel. The last thing in my grab bag of shame was my lab coat. I pulled it out and tossed it in the washer, but as I did, I heard a clanking sound. Unenthusiastically retrieving the lab coat, I patted it down. I assumed it was keys from the lab or loose change, but that's when I realized I forgot about the two blood-filled vacutainers I slid in my pocket a few days earlier.

When I was thirteen or fourteen years old, I was at the Quik-Mart a few blocks from my childhood home with some neighborhood friends. While we were waiting in line to pay for our chocolate bars and sodas with our weekly allowance, the woman in front of me dropped a twenty-dollar bill. She carried a small child in one arm while she pressed a few products—carton of milk, some lunch meats, and a loaf of bread—in the other arm against her chest as she fumbled with her purse one-handed. She didn't notice she had dropped the money, and me being an angsty teenage boy, swooped in and snatched the twenty and shoved it in my pocket before she could figure out what had happened.

When it was her turn at the counter, she placed the products down and continued to search her purse. With each second, she grew more frantic. The salesclerk turned her away and she stormed out of the store with tears trailing down her cheeks. My buddies and I paid for our snacks and stepped outside to find her sitting on the curb, child in her lap, and her purse dumped on the oil-stained concrete.

The rest of my pals hopped on their bikes and took off; we had plans to go play one of their brand-new video game systems. I told them I would meet them there. I stood behind the woman, my hand in my pocket squeezing the twenty-dollar bill. I wanted to give it back to her, but I had never possessed that much money before—it was quadruple my weekly allowance. For what had to have been fifteen or twenty minutes, I stood there and watched her cry. I never returned the money.

I felt a sense of guilt that day.

I felt a sense of power, too.

I hadn't felt that strange cocktail of emotions again, until now.

I paced back and forth in the glorified nook I called a dining room; my eyes locked on the two vacutainers that sat on the table. Like the distant rumble of an inbound train, the mantra returned.

There is an urge inside you which cannot be satisfied with conventional methods.

It grew louder and louder and my mouth started to salivate. I didn't mean to steal the blood samples, the less-than-an-ounce of blood within them was not going to stifle the livelihood of the people they came from either. If anything, it would be a slap on the wrist and a lot of catch up at work. Nevertheless, I felt that childhood guilt. I tasted the power I felt that day.

The being, the _god_, returned to my body, but this time it did not kick me out. The very presence of it weighed me down, every muscle in my body losing the battle to gravity. The being did not take me over completely, instead, it nudged me. Periodic boosts of energy had my legs and arms jerk violently like a dying insect as it led me to the table. It helped me wrap my bony fingers around one of the vacutainers and twist open the cap. The vacutainer lurched toward my lips, and I peered down my nose at the contents that had taken on a muddy-brown hue.

The being brought me this far, now it was up to me to decide. I pressed the broken seal of the vacutainer to my lips and sucked. The blood felt like mucus on my tongue.

I jerked my head back and sucked harder, like a sorority girl downing a Jell-O shot. The contents crept down my throat and I breathed deep through my nose.

I was no longer hungry.

I felt like I was floating.

FIVE

*G*od was the best way to describe this entity. It didn't take on a form, that is, except my own. It didn't have its own physical features, but I could sense a personality.

It was a force, invisible, but distinct like the wind. Like water conforming to its container. Tectonic plates under the surface. Its sentience experienced vicariously through my senses. The Plato to my Aristotle. Miyagi to my Daniel. The lantern in the darkness that is life, highlighting checkpoints along the long winding trail, providing guidance, direction, and purpose.

I don't recall what exactly happened after I sucked down the contents of that first vacutainer, but I do remember waking up the next day in my bed. I slept like a stoned fucking baby. Revitalized. Sharp. Ready to conquer the day.

I showered, I shaved, I put a little bit of

pomade in my hair and messed it up in such a way that it covered most of the baldness plaguing the crown of my cranium. Instead of the wrinkled, neutral colored button-up I'd usually throw on, *we* decided to be bold.

I searched my closet, the further back I went, the more ancient the relics. Somewhere in the mid-nineties, I stopped and plucked a vibrant green, dog's tooth patterned button-up off the rack. I found the perfect floral, art nouveau style necktie made up of silky purples and yellows that complimented the shirt.

The drive to work was nice. I left the windows rolled down partly to feel the winter breeze in my hair, but mostly to air out the cab of my car. I forgot about that portion of "the incident". It was early morning on a Saturday, so traffic was minimal. I think I even caught a glimpse of the sun through a tear in the blanket of ash-colored clouds.

When I arrived at the hospital, I decided to make my way in through the E.R. Waiting Room rather than the employee entrance in the back. Strutting through the halls, the nurses—even some male ones—gasped and raised their eyebrows as I rolled by. There was a bounce in my step. There was a shimmer in my eye.

I was the toucan among pigeons.

The bright red apple in Jonas' hand.

The rainbow in hell.

Showing up to work with no intention to do any, I spent roughly twenty minutes prancing down the halls like a peacock, fishing for reactions. For the first time in a long time, I yearned to be noticed, strived to be the focus of attention, rather than bury my head in the sand and wait for the day to be over.

I relished every moment until I turned the corner and spotted Dr. Geraldo and Wendy. I pivoted on my heels and headed back to the other side of the corner. I leaned into the wall with my shoulder and poked my head around.

He said something and they shared a laugh. They smiled at each other, that is when it occurred to me that I've never seen Dr. Geraldo with any expression other than a scowl on his chiseled face. Wendy tilted her head down, and with her murky green eyes, peered up at him through her brow, her bottom lip under her teeth. She reached out and softly clasped his forearm and giggled. Dr. Geraldo placed his hand on top of hers.

"Dr. Phillips?" A voice at the bottom of a well said. "Hello?"

When I came to, I was standing in front of Dr. Geraldo and Wendy. Unsurprisingly, they both shared the same concerned expression.

"Oh," I muttered, "hello."

"Are you feeling better?" Wendy asked.

"Wendy told me all about the other day," Dr. Geraldo said, not half a second after Wendy asked her question. "Sounds like you came down with a bad case of the flu."

The blood rushed back to my head, and I felt a tinge of vertigo. "I..."

"Don't worry, Gary," Dr. Geraldo raised his palm as if he were halting traffic, "Wendy and I made sure to put a dent in your workload. We knew you had fallen behind and didn't want you to stress out about it while you recovered from your illness. However, there is still work to be done, but just the usual amount."

"Well..." I was at a loss for words. His smile was condescending. I'm sure that whole exchange would have gone down differently if it weren't for Wendy standing by his side. "Thank you."

"Say, weren't you not supposed to be back until tomorrow?" Wendy asked.

"Yeah," I said. "I was feeling better, but not so much anymore. I may just head back home."

Wendy's responded with an exaggerated frown.

"Then we'll see you tomorrow," Dr. Geraldo said. He glanced at his wristwatch before wrenching his head to look past me down the hall. "Okay, I've got to get going. Feel better, Dr. Phillips. Oh, and by the way, you clean up well. Nice tie."

I nodded. I came here seeking positive attention, and I got it, even from the Devil himself. It felt wrong. It felt forced. It made me angry.

Wendy waited until Dr. Geraldo turned the corner, when he did, her giddy demeanor faded.

"When I first told Dr. Geraldo about you taking a few days off, he was livid." Wendy exhaled as though she was holding her breath the whole time. "I calmed him down, used my charm, told him the other phlebotomists and I would pick up the slack while you were gone." She winked at me and all my extremities started to tingle.

He just wants to fuck you, I thought.

"What?" She said as she narrowed her eyes.

Shit. I must have said it out loud. "What?"

"You just mumbled something."

"Oh... I said..." Shit. "I said *he's such a fucking tool.*"

Wendy was silent for a moment too long

before she released a delicate chuckle. "Yeah," she chuckled some more, "I thought you said something else."

Change the subject.

"So, is everything okay?" I scratched the side of my head.

"I'm fine."

"With the lab?"

"Why wouldn't it be?"

"I don't know."

To say the silence was awkward would be like saying fire is hot.

"So—"

"I'm gonna go back home," I blurted. "I still feel a little out of it."

"Okay, Dr. Phillips," Wendy forced a smile. "I'll see you tomorrow."

I returned the smile and began to skulk back whence I came when she said, "By the way, you're looking very dapper today." I turned around and she waved goodbye, "Feel better, Gary."

I couldn't even make it home. I scurried to the nearest restroom, fortunately one with a single toilet and lock on the door, dropped my pants and went to *The Beach*. I visited *The Beach* so often, the photos were cached on my phone and basically loaded before I could press the button. My eyes darted from the cluster of freckles above her left breast to the flower tattoo on her right hip. They traveled from her eyes to her lips, down to her wet, white bikini top and back up again like the pixel bouncing from paddle to paddle in *Pong*.

Twenty minutes.

Twenty fucking minutes, I tried. But there was something else. Something diverting my attention like a pebble in my shoe.

Dr. Geraldo stood behind her, his hands clasped Wendy's hips. His well-defined chin rested on her shoulder. His stupid fucking face was smiling. He looked me straight in the eyes, mocking me.

I closed the photo and reopened it more times than I care to count, but he was still there. I sat on the toilet, pants around my ankles, phone in one hand, my chaffed, flaccid self in the other while I tried to make him go away. I tried another photo, but he was there.

Another, and there he was.

I contemplated pornography, but the hospital's wi-fi was shit. And the thought of finishing to another woman wasn't any more appealing than having Dr. Geraldo stare me in the face while I tried to pleasure myself.

I stood and pulled up my pants, but they weighed a lot more than when I sat down. My stomach rumbled. Darkness bled into the edges of my vision creating a vignette of reality. My arms shook violently as I buckled my belt, but it wasn't *me* doing it.

God had taken over again, but this time it was going to let me spectate. It was like a dream, a dream where you are aware you are dreaming. That familiar feeling of treading through a swimming pool, fully aware of the forces pushing against your body. I was somewhere between floating and sinking, bobbing really, as I sat as a passenger in my own skin.

We entered the lab, fortunately for me it was empty. Being a Saturday, there was essentially a skeleton crew that carried out the menial duties, and it just happened to be their lunch break. Everything important would wait until Monday. We floated straight to the refrigerator that housed the vacutainers of blood samples, opened it, snatched a couple, pocketed them, and floated out unseen.

SIX

It was a few minutes after five in the evening when full control was returned to me. The winter sun sank behind the cityscape leaving the horizon a silhouette of skyscrapers and painting the drab, gray overcast with hues of dirty pinks and purples.

It would be dark soon. And the night was young.

After we snatched the blood samples from the lab, I sat idly by as my body sauntered through the hospital. A few nurses waved as I passed, but God must've chalked it up as unimportant because we just floated by them without so much as making eye contact.

I must admit I was nervous when we got behind the wheel of my car and turned the ignition. My heart fell into my stomach when the engine revved and my vehicle erratically backed out of the parking spot almost smashing into a truck parked in the adjacent row.

The drive was smooth enough apart from the abrupt stops and aggressive accelerations at every stoplight. We weren't headed home, rather we ended up in a parking garage near Third Street and Hauser. Third Street and Hauser was one end of a stretch of city blocks fraught with bars, dance clubs, and strip joints: the nightlife Mecca of Claybrook City.

God reached in my inside Member's Only jacket pocket and retrieved the two vacutainers, and, in quick succession, knocked them back. Double dosage. I would equate the freshness to sushi. These were straight out of the sea, sliced, rolled, and served. Whereas my first experience was equivalent to three days expired gas station sushi that had been sitting on a dusty shelf, unrefrigerated. I could even taste hints of adenine and sodium di-phosphate, a few of the chemicals put in the blood that helped preserve it during storage.

Like a computer coming online, I could feel the power surge back into my limbs and fingers. The haze dissipated and the world was as clear as it had ever been.

I started my crawl at *Jackie's Bar & Grill* on the southeast corner of Third Street and Hauser. It was a tame place; a middle-class establishment where children can enjoy their reheated chicken fingers and use brittle, recycled crayons to destroy their paper table mats while the parents could drink their drinks, watch the game, or play pop culture trivia on the bulky handheld devices.

I sat at a bar top, sipped on a cat piss domestic, and scanned the room, observing the patrons. Some families, mostly groups of bachelors pregaming before they head out to the clubs, and a few middle-aged married couples attempting to relish the few hours of freedom before they had to return home to their shitty kids and pay their overpriced babysitter.

Besides me, the only other *lone wolf* in the joint was a gray-bearded vet. His black hat adorned with an array of military insignias, one of which being the 9th Infantry Division—the same division Francis was in. He sat at the end of the bar, his head cocked up as he watched the hockey game displayed on the television that hung above him.

I wasn't sure how long I had been staring at him, but he turned to look at me. Big, yellow letters that read "Vietnam Veteran" took up the whole front of his cap. He stared at me with his dead eyes and tilted his head a degree like a curious puppy. It was like he knew what I was. What *we* were. What I, *we*, have been doing. I saw Francis in him. His rugged features masked by his bushy beard. A deluge of memories I didn't want to remember flooded my head.

Growing up, I couldn't help but always fuck up... At least in the eyes of Francis. Every day was punishment. Hugging the big oak tree in the yard while Francis lashed my bare back with his rawhide leather belt because I forgot to fold his laundry. Every time I forgot "Sir" when addressing him was a swift slap to my jaw; they weren't always openhanded.

One day, when I was fourteen, I didn't make my bed before leaving for school. When I returned home, I found my pillow out in the yard under the same oak tree. Francis said if I can't maintain my bed, I don't deserve one. He beat me and threw me outside. He called me an animal and fed me cold, canned beans in a dog bowl. I slept outside that night. It was the first snow of the season.

"You got a problem, boy?" The vet swiveled on his barstool to face me.

"Not at all, sir." I walked over to him. "I just noticed the 9th Infantry Division insignia on your hat. My grandpa was a part of that division."

"Well, no shit?" What's the name?"

I saw a glimpse of his toothless smile under his beard.

"Sergeant Phillips. Sergeant Francis K. Phillips."

The dirty vet's eyes rolled upward as he pondered. "Doesn't ring a bell."

"Well," I said, "I just wanted to thank you for your service."

That place was killing my groove. I paid my bill and got out.

I jumped from establishment to establishment. The further down the street, the less tame they became. Yet, within every one of them I found myself sitting in the corner by myself, brooding with my beer as I watched the people let loose. Every lonesome woman was out of my league and didn't look like they wanted to be bothered by the likes of me. Every woman I may have had a chance with was accompanied by a male. Even if I had the chance, I don't think I would be able to initiate contact. It had been far too long, a decade really, since I'd been physically intimate with another, which wasn't intimate at all.

It was an average girl I met in one of those online dating chatrooms. She was a single mother; her name was Lisa. I took her to the cliché dinner and a movie, and I assumed I didn't fuck it up too bad because she agreed to some drinks afterwards. Somewhere between second and third base at her place, she either wised up or sobered up or both, because she asked me to leave. I'm not sure what I did, but I never saw her again. I haven't been on a date since.

I wasn't finding any luck inside, so I decided to get some fresh air.

Packs of people roamed the street. The buildings were lined with Christmas lights and neon signs that reflected off the rain slicked pavement and asphalt bestowing on the world a dark glow like an eighties sci-fi movie. The cacophony of bass and excited chatter poured out from the various bars and clubs only lent itself to that setting. Reinforcing it.

I went with it.

At that moment, I felt like Rick Deckard aimlessly perusing the busy streets of a corporate dystopia. I cut through the herds of pedestrians, waving my shallow, yet cocksure, grin like it was a banner. The quiet sprinkle evolved into pellet-sized droplets and the traffic on the sidewalk retreated inside the various establishments. The ones that refused to put out their cigarettes found refuge under the awnings. I kept walking.

My soaked head high and my hands casually tucked in my jacket pockets. I had a surge of determination. I oozed tenacity. Yet, when I questioned myself as to why that was, I stopped in my tracks as though I'd reached the edge of the world.

Where was I going?

My fingers felt as though they were caked in liquid cement. My head was unbalanced on my neck and swayed side to side. Time for a course correction. Enough of my meandering. We pivoted on my heels and strutted south, away from Hauser.

About a dozen blocks south of Hauser is when the neighborhoods really started turning to shit. Like a time-lapse video of a decaying flower, the further I walked, the corrosion of Claybrook City progressively revealed itself. The rain had subsided back into a light sprinkle. Stray dogs wandered in packs. Humans did too. Hoodies drawn, heads down, they crept in the shadows and alleyways.

People hollered obscenities from their second, third, and fourth story windows at the pedestrians below and each other.

It was at Moore Street when I saw them. Four women stood on the corner with far more revealing attire than any normal civilian might wear during a rainy winter night. As I approached them, they solicited me. That took care of one thing I worried about: how to go about asking.

If I can recall correctly, there was Raquel, Love, Snowflake, and Jasmine. Love, a thick, busty blonde with bright blue lipstick initiated contact as I neared. "Hey, Sugar," she said, exhaling the smoke from her cigarette. "Looking for some fun tonight?"

I nodded.

Raquel, Love, and Jasmine all shot me smiles and perked up their breasts. "Alright, baby," Love said, "it's a hundred an hour. Where is this happening? I don't see a car."

"There a hotel nearby?" I asked.

"Two blocks south," Raquel said. "Dirty, cheap, and always a vacant room." She stepped forward and ran her fingernails down the side of my neck.

I twitched.

Snowflake leaned against the graffiti riddled building wall behind them, one leg perched behind her, and looked disinterested in the negotiations. Her face was pockets of black ice on snow. Thick black lipstick and mascara made her pale skin radiant under the streetlights. She wore a black leather biker's jacket, and her cleavage tested the seams of her midnight purple blouse. Her skirt and knee-high, lace-up boots, too, were black; her stockings matched the blouse.

"What about her?" I pointed at Snowflake with my chin.

"Who? Snowflake?"

"Sure. I guess."

"*Shark week*." Raquel said.

"Huh?"

"*Aunt Flo.*"

Before I had the chance to acknowledge that I understood, Love continued where Raquel left off. "*Crimson Tide. Cousin Red.* She's *on the blob.*"

"Yeah, I get it."

My heart pounded and the *hunger* came back. Vacutainers was one thing, but I wasn't sure about this. I spoke nonetheless, not sure if it was under my own volition or not.

"Snowflake," I muttered, "want to get out of

here?"

She didn't seem too thrilled at the idea, but work is work. She led me to the roach motel a few blocks farther south. Thirty cash scored me a room for the night.

SEVEN

The room stunk with sour bodily fluids and stale cigarette smoke. It was obvious that the place once had carpeting, but that had been crudely torn out leaving the cold, cracked cement exposed. There was queen-sized spring mattress bed on a rusty steel frame and a box television complete with a dial; something I haven't seen since my childhood. There were bars on the window, although the view from it was the side of the neighboring building only a few yards away. The wallpaper had once been a vibrant white with floral design, but now it was peeling and stained with browns and yellows. If I didn't catch anything from the prostitute or the dirty bed sheets, I'd sure as hell be affected by the black mold growing in the walls. Overall, it may as well have been an upscale jail cell.

The hotel, suitably named *Lucky's Suites,* existed for two reasons: drugs and fucking. I was about to engage in both.

Snowflake didn't say a word to me during the walk to the hotel. She didn't make a peep as we climbed the stairs to the fourth floor. She didn't so much as look in my direction when we entered the room. The first thing she did was retrieve a little white baggy inside her bra and lay out a line on top of the television.

I stood in the doorway, not sure how this worked. I had never purchased sex before.

Do I ask?

Or do I just take off my pants?

Snowflake took one of the bills I paid her with, rolled it up, and snorted the line. She wiggled her nose like Samantha from *Bewitched* and cleared her throat as she removed her leather jacket. She looked at me and, with her head, motioned toward the rickety bed. There was a lump in my throat.

"Mind if I try some?" I squeaked.

"Huh?" She raised an eyebrow.

"Mind if I try some of that coke?" The bag was on top of the box television. I pointed at it.

She pursed her lips and squinted at the baggie

like she was doing calculus in her head.

"It's gonna cost you," she said. "Shit isn't free."

Her voice was soft and high and, for the first time, it dawned on me how young she actually was. I don't know how one falls into this life, or if this is how life has always been for them. I stopped pondering and pushed my morality to the back of my brain. This is not the time nor place to empathize.

"Of course." I pulled out my wallet and snatched some bills. "Is fifty enough?"

She licked her lips, walked over to me, and snatched the money from my shaky hand. She grabbed my tie, turned around, led me to the television and cut me a line.

Before the numbness could take over my sinuses, she grabbed me by the belt buckle, walked me to the foot of the bed, and pushed me onto it. My knees bent over the edge, she stood between them, the outside of her thighs grazing the inside of mine. Her face was blank, the emptiness a face expresses during mindless routine; she may as well have been doing her laundry. She crossed her arms, latched onto the bottom of her blouse, and peeled it off over her head. She unlatched her bra and freed her breasts.

I held my breath. My heart raced, I could hear it pounding in my ears.

She lowered herself to her knees and unfastened my belt while her big, blue eyes stared up at mine gawking down at her. That alone almost made me finish.

She tugged on my pants and briefs until I was exposed. She squeezed me tight in her hand.

The warmth of my member felt unbelievably incredible against her small, frigid palm and I could feel my blood pulsating against her grip. It sent chills down my legs and up my arms. My fingers and toes became numb with excitement. I felt the all-to-familiar wave of euphoria wash over me. I clinched my gluteus maximus and whatever fucking muscle people talk about when they talk about *kegels*, but I lost control.

"Hmm..." Snowflake muttered. "You might have broken the record." She wiped my shame off her chest with the mustard-colored cotton blanket.

"Oh, fuck me. I'm sorry." I couldn't even look at her. I just laid there and stared at the ceiling. "It's been a while."

"Don't apologize to me." She stood up and cut herself another line on top of the television. "You still have forty-five minutes, give or take, what you wanna do now is up to you."

I wasn't sure what to say. However, God had a few ideas.

When the numbness started to recede and as I regained feeling back in my sinuses, the metallic taste of dirty pennies that coated my tongue grew stronger. I'm not entirely sure how long I'd been down below, but I knew I had well exceeded my hour. God handed me the reins a few minutes after we started; this was all me now. Snowflake didn't seem to mind all that much. Actually, she was somewhat surprised at the request. She told me she wasn't one to turn down pleasure, plus, I paid the fee. She said she's heard stranger requests.

If the first taste a few days ago was wretched, gas station sushi, and the two vacutainers I sucked down in my car earlier that evening was fresh sushi; at this moment, I was a Great White Shark roaming the coast of a crowded beach on a fucking feeding frenzy.

She squeezed her thighs tight around my head, compressing my ears into the sides of my skull, and I could hear the ocean. She arched her back and held her breath. The muscles in her legs and stomach trembled. With one hand, she latched onto the back of my head and forced my face deeper into her loins, mashing my nose against her pubic bone. Her other hand clawed at the side of the bed. I couldn't breathe, but I didn't stop.

Finally, she exhaled a high-pitch moan, relaxed her muscles, and released my head from her tentacle-like grip. But I still didn't stop.

"Okay," she said, out of breath, "I'm done."

I kept going.

She scooted back on the mattress and sat up against the headboard.

The urge to growl like a Rottweiler swelled up in my throat, but I fought it. I took a deep breath, licked the crimson from my lips, and wiped my slimy face on the blanket next to my shame. I stood up and experienced a bout of vertigo as the blood rushed to my brain. I stumbled for a moment and caught myself on the edge of the bed. I sat down, closed my eyes, and stretched my jaw which created a clicking noise in my mandibular notch.

"You doin' okay there?" She lit a cigarette. I didn't even see where she got it from. She held out the pack, flipped it open, and offered me one. I indulged and she lit it for me.

"Yeah." I took a drag from the cigarette and erupted into a fit of coughs. After I caught my breath, I wheezed, "I feel fucking fantastic."

"You're a freak, you know that?"

"I..." I cleared my throat. The taste of her bloody nether regions still dominated my mouth. "I'm sorry."

"It's not a bad thing." She stood up, retrieved her stockings from the cold cement. The cigarette dangling between her lips and her exposed breasts bounced in sync as she wiggled into them and her boots. She threw on her blouse and jacket and sauntered to the television where the cocaine still resided. "Do you want another line before I go?" Her voice was friendly. "It's on the house."

"Sure."

She emptied the baggie on the television and cut two lines. She ripped open the bag, exposing the inside, and licked it clean. I snorted my portion and passed her the bill and she did the same. She sniffled and ran her tongue across her front teeth.

"Okay then." Snowflake nodded at me and headed toward the door.

"Hey," I said, forcing her to stop and face me. "I have the room for the night if you want to stay."

Her smile seemed genuine, until she laughed.

"Not how this works," She sighed. "I gotta get back out there."

I turned and glanced out the window. "But it's raining."

"*Neither snow nor rain nor heat nor gloom of night*," She said in mockingly official tone. "Someone's gonna pay to get their cock stroked." She turned back to the door and grabbed the handle.

"Will I see you again?" I asked.

"If you have the cash," She said without turning to look at me, "you know where to find me." The door closed behind her.

I was alone.

I sat on the edge of the bed in silence and waited for God to return.

What do I do now?

I was full—like, buffet full. The thought of blood brought on nausea as vodka would during a hellish hangover. The strange thing was, I felt great—physically. Hunger satisfied and chalk full of energy, and that's not including the influence of the drugs. I was lost.

Where was God?

What should I do?

I analyzed the faded, peeling pattern on the wall for almost an hour before deciding I needed to get some fresh air.

I sauntered to the bathroom and observed my face in the spider webbed mirror. I resembled a toddler who had just annihilated a red popsicle. Using the miniature bar of soap that crumbled apart as soon as I touched it, I washed Snowflake's stains from my cheeks, chin, lips, and bridge and tip of my nose.

I peered out the caged window as I slipped into my jacket. It was still raining, but I didn't care.

I didn't know where I was going, but I didn't want to stay there.

I had walked for a while with no destination. I deliberated returning home. Deliberated finding Snowflake and coughing up the dough for a few more hours of her time. I didn't necessarily want to for the sex, although I wouldn't neglect the act if it were to arise, but being alone for the first time, after being intimate with someone after a long time, was crippling. Even if the intimacy was all business and even if any sliver of genuine interest in me I thought I saw in her was a convincing façade, the warmth of another human being was irreplaceable.

So, I walked.

It had to be sometime around three in the morning. There was a chilly breeze that wafted through the streets, causing loose trash and dead leaves to tumble, and the pitter-patter of the rain on the sidewalk emulated the sound of footsteps and kept me constantly looking over my shoulder.

I turned down a narrow alleyway, the roofs of the neighboring buildings jutted out just enough to provide some refuge from the drizzle as long as I stayed close to the wall. As I traversed further down the alleyway, the glow from the streetlights faded away.

The only source of light was a few blocks in front of me where the alleyway spat back out into a street. I stopped and leaned against the wall and looked in both directions, the exits were equal distances apart. I raised my hand to wipe away the soaked bangs that clung to my forehead and I couldn't see my palm a few inches from my face.

I was in the belly of this abyss.

I basked in my own aphotic realm.

The darkness was oddly reassuring, like the embrace of a mother. It was strange that my mind chalked it up to that; however, the concept of it was both foreign and familiar. I don't remember my mother, and I sure as hell have never been embraced by Francis.

I see it at the hospital all the time: A scared

child grasps for their mother's arms. The calm that takes over their expressions as they nuzzle their head into their loving mother's bosom. Or that panicked mother that rushes into the hospital after receiving news of their child's injury at school, the first thing she needs is the comfort of her *baby's* head against her heart, letting them both know that everything is going to be okay.

I wondered if my mother felt that way about me. I wondered if she thought about me the moment before her death. Did she think about how she wouldn't be able to hold me close and watch me grow? Did she even have *that* moment before she died? Francis told me it was a car crash, but the more I thought about it, the more I realized how little I knew about it. Where were they going? Was I in the car? If not, where was I?

Maybe I was told and forgot. Maybe it didn't matter. The more I thought about it, the angrier I became. My fingers went numb and my head grew heavy. God had a plan, but this time I fought its invasion. Their brief interjection came and went and I retained control. The sun had started to rise, and I wasn't ready for another adventure.

It was time to go home.

EIGHT

I decided to head straight for my car that still sat in the parking garage by Third Street and Hauser. Of course, I forgot my keys in the fucking hotel room. The trot back to the hotel from my car and then back again was an eternity.

When I arrived home, I was surprised to find Francis not in the recliner but still asleep and snoring in his room. Usually, by this time, he'd be up and already a few beers deep, searching for any reason to give me hell. I made sure to be as silent as possible as I closed the front door and tip-toed upstairs like a ninja.

Most days I could only hope Francis was unconscious when I returned home, however, for the better part of the morning I'd been brooding about the unanswered questions when it came to my deceased parents. I wanted to clarify some things about their death with Francis but waking him was never worth the trouble. The only thing that I would receive would be a slew of insults and possibly a few swings for my jaw. Best wait until later.

I was due back at the hospital in a few hours. Reeking like the hotel room and then some, I took a quick shower, fixed up my hair, and picked out a plaid button-up made up of various shades of maroon. I found the flat black tie I wore to a co-worker's funeral awhile back to go with it. I debated wearing my glasses, but instead just put in a new pair of contact lenses since the lack of my bifocals received such positive attention the day before.

After cleaning up, I had just a smidge over an hour before I had to leave for work. I was still *full* of Snowflake, so I wasn't hungry. My mother's manuscript was still scattered about my room, so I decided it was a better time than any to wrangle them up.

The process was tedious. None of the pages were in order, so much of the time was spent searching for page numbers. The last half of the damned thing was a jumble of incomprehensible garbage that, of course, had no page numbers; that made it a bit easier. Anytime I found a page that didn't look formatted correctly and didn't have a page number, I set it aside in its own stack.

I was almost done compiling chapter three when I saw the mantra. It was hidden within the nonsense, and caught my eye like a bloodstain on a white carpet:

DENIGAM TATHWTONS IEESITAHTUBS **THERE IS AN URGE INSIDE YOU THAT CANNOT BE SATISFIED WITH CONVENTIONAL MENTHODS** SKITHGIN DORGOASRSD KOOQENDSEI DANSOIGS.....?????

I went back and checked another *nonsense* page. There it was again; mixed into the fray of randomness but was clear as day. I checked another. And another. Every one of them had the mantra.

The Mantra.

Was this something subliminal?

My eyes must've scanned it before while reading—or at the very least—eyeballing the nonsense pages.

But why?

Why did this have to do with the lack of a

better word, "*possessions*"?

What did this have to do with the blood?

Blood. My stomach rumbled and turned, and the inside of my mouth was as arid as the Sonora. My fingers went numb.

Thinking of what I was told about the death of my parents, only a single detail came to mind: Car wreck. Nothing else. The vagueness of it all ate at my psyche and my temporal arteries pulsated against my skull. There was only one person who was able to provide me with closure. Nap time was over, Francis.

I stormed downstairs and into the master bedroom located on the other side of the living room. Funny how I paid the rent, the utilities, and all other amenities, but I got stuffed upstairs in the tiny guest bedroom.

He laid on one side, closest to the door, of the king size bed he forced me to buy him, still snoring.

I front-kicked the side of the mattress and knocked over his prosthetic leg that leaned against it. "Wake up!"

His eyes shot open, staring straight at the ceiling as if his brain were still powering up. Without moving his head, his eyes darted to me. My shoulders hunched, I towered over the side of his bed. For a moment, I think the only moment, Francis seemed shaken and nervous. His nostrils flared as he inhaled deep through his nose and the air laboring to advance past his collapsed septum made a whistling sound like a shy teapot.

The familiar irritation returned to his eyes as they glossed over, "What the fuck do you want, Gary?"

"What happened to my mother?"

Francis' face was blank. He raised an eyebrow in confusion. "What the fuck are you talking about?"

"Mom…" I swallowed the cotton ball that had formed in my throat. "And Dad."

"Are ya' fuckin' high, dipshit?" Francis said. "They're dead."

"No shit." I barked. "How did they die?"

"I don't know how many times I gotta fuckin' tell you," Francis said. He sat up against the headboard. The blanket slid down to his lap; he pulled at it and nestled it under his beer gut. The crudely inked 9th Infantry Division insignia tattoo was faded and blotchy and sat on his left, stretch marked breast. "It was a car accident."

"Who was driving?"

"Um…" The hesitation was suspicious.

"Cynthia. Your mother."

"And where was I?"

"You were..." Francis trailed off. "Uh—"

"See! You've told me they died in a car wreck, but I've never dug, never asked any fucking questions. You wanna know why?" I didn't give him time to answer. "Because I was always answered with silence, neglect, and abuse. If that were the actual truth, why are you so goddamn vague? What are you hiding?"

Francis lips parted as if he were going to speak, but he didn't. So, I continued.

"Your fucking son, your *only* fucking son, my father, died that day too. You should know every fucking detail of that day. That day should haunt you, it should torment you, and you have trouble recalling simple fucking details? I fuckin—"

"It does fuckin' haunt me, Gary!" Francis erupted. His bulldog jowls shook as he spoke. "You wanna fuckin' know, do you? Ya' want to fuckin' know the truth about the death of my only son and that psycho whore wife of his you call a mother?"

Psycho whore!? I struck a nerve. There was something. I was speechless. I clenched my jaw and nodded.

"Your father was a hell of a man, Gary. Far

better than I ever was." Francis looked me up and down. "And far better than you'll ever be. He was steadily climbing the ranks within the police department. An honest, tough, hardworking man.

"Your mother on the other hand..." Francis shook his head, I swear I could hear his teeth grinding. "Was unemployed. Self-righteous, too. Your father was a good man, but somehow, some fuckin' how, he was just dumb enough to love your mother."

"What was wrong with my mother?"

"She was crazy," Francis said nonchalantly. "At first, I thought... I blew it off as the *normal* crazy, you know? The *has too many shots at the bar* crazy. The *runs her mouth at the wrong time crazy*. Those are the ones that usually fuck the best, so I didn't hound on your father too much for fallin' for her. She told everyone she was a writer. Yet do you see any fuckin' books with her name on it?"

I didn't notice until now, but I had one of the nonsense pages still in my hand; wrinkled up in my balled fist. "What are you getting at?"

"The bitch grew resentful."

"What?"

"With your father working all the time, I spent

a good amount over at the house. I watched you, bathed you, played with you, fed you. This was at the request of your father, who told me he couldn't come home without facing a tantrum from the cunt. Just to give Cynthia some space. She used to sit in front of the fuckin' typewriter and stare off. I swear to fuckin' god I've never even seen her use the damn thing. Just sit in front of it and stare at the blank, white page."

"How did they die?"

"You know you remind me of her." Francis ignored my question. "The way you look, the way you live, even the way you speak. I tried to mold you into something respectable. Hell, I tried to beat it out of you, but it just wouldn't take. Do you know what it is like to look at your fucking face for decades and see the woman who killed my son?"

My heart was entangled in my intestines. "My mother killed my father?"

"Your father called me one night and asked me if I could babysit you so he could take Cynthia out for a much needed 'date night,'" Francis continued as if he didn't just drop an atom bomb on my reality. "I agreed. You know, there was a time when I loved you, Gary."

My vision blurred.

I blinked.

A steady stream of tears rolled down my cheeks.

"It was a summer night. It had to be eight or nine 'o'clock and it was still hotter than hell outside. I pulled up to the house..." Francis cleared his throat. "You'll see why I didn't want to live there. I pulled up to the house and made my way inside. All the lights in the house were on, so was the television in the living room, but there was no sign of anyone.

"I grabbed a beer from the fridge and sat on the couch. I figured Thomas and Cynthia were still getting ready and you were napping, I didn't want to walk down the hall and bother any of you. So, I sat there, must've been fifteen minutes, and watched whatever shitty sitcom was on until I heard your voice. You had just turned two, so the majority of what you said was babblin' and broken English. But I heard you, babblin' away down the hall. I was surprised not to hear Thomas or Cynthia respond to you. You babbled on for the better half of a minute. Something seemed off about that, so I went to investigate..."

Francis lowered his gaze and ran his palms down his face as he exhaled. He cleared his throat and whispered something.

"What did you say?" I bellowed.

Francis, again, whispered it to himself.

"What the fuck are you saying?"

"I should have just fuckin' left you there." Francis said as he stared at his lap. He gradually returned his focus to me. "I stood in the doorway to your parent's room. There she was, Cynthia, your mother, she'd hung herself from one of the wooden beams that ran across the ceiling. She was naked, covered in blood. She was facin' me and her eyes were wide open, bulgin' and lookin' straight at me as she swayed back and forth.

"Your father was—" The knot in Francis throat was evident and tears swelled up in his eyes. "Thomas, my boy, my only son, had his wrists and ankles tied to the bedpost. He was naked, too, covered in blood. There was a white washcloth shoved in his mouth. His body was pockmarked with bite marks and stab wounds..."

"I—"

"The police said it was a murder-suicide. Your psycho whore of a mother stabbed my son over forty times with a pair of scissors."

"Where..." My head was a three-ton boulder resting on top of my twig of a neck. My knees were glass and ready to shatter. "Where was I?"

"You were there." Francis' face grew red.

I wasn't sure if he was about to laugh, scream, or weep. It was the kind of expression that was a precursor to an emotional outburst. I just wasn't sure what kind.

"You were there on the floor. Directly underneath Cynthia's limp, danglin' legs. You were layin' on your back, eyes wide open and locked on your mother's body that gently swung back and forth. You were gigglin' as the blood from her body that ran down her legs and dripped off her toes onto you."

A barrage of imagery flickered through my mind. I wasn't sure if I was picturing what Francis described or if they were genuine, repressed memories finally breaking the surface.

There was an awful silence. Only the sound of us both breathing heavily in staggered succession broke the calm.

"I wish she would have killed you too," Francis said as he threw the blanket off his lower torso. He massaged his knee that sat just above his stump. He leaned on his elbow and reached toward my feet off the edge of the bed, blindly grasping for his prosthetic leg I had knocked over. After a few feeble attempts to reach it, he sat back up against the headboard and sighed. "You mind givin' me a hand, ya' little shit?"

It all happened so very fast.

I bent down and retrieved the rigid plastic and resin prosthetic leg and without hesitation I struck Francis in the face.

Then, I did it again.

And again.

And then I stopped counting.

With each blow, his nose sank deeper and deeper into his skull. If he screamed, if he cried, if he made any noise during my fusillade, I wasn't aware.

When I was done, my forearm and bicep ached. Francis' face resembled a raspberry pie that had been pummeled by a hammer. There was a faint gurgling emanating from his throat. If he wasn't dead yet, he would be soon; but I wasn't going to stick around to watch him go.

I was running late for work.

NINE

I should've had an unbearable amount of guilt.
I should've had at least a sliver of it.
I didn't.

Each time I brought the prosthetic leg down on Francis' face, it had more force than the last. Each time, more cathartic. For so long, I was underwater. Running out of breath, I couldn't tell what was up or down. Shattering Francis' face was breaking the surface. I could finally breathe again.

"Well, you look like you're feeling better." I didn't realize Wendy had entered the lab.

I was sitting at my desk; my eyes must have been glossed over as I was reliving what I had just done. My cheeks hurt, unaware I had been smiling.

"Fantastic." I jerked my head to face her.

Wendy replied with a smile of her own.

The day drifted by in a haze while I replayed

the event in my head. I fantasized about what I could have done differently. What else could I have done to inflict even a portion of the suffering Francis had caused me throughout my life? Maybe I should have beat his remaining leg to a pulp and watch him writhe in pain. I could have used a more efficient tool for the job, like a hammer. There had to be a hammer somewhere in the garage along with Francis' other unnecessary collection of maintenance crap. I swear I've seen a few hammers in there. I did, however, own and know the location of a meat tenderizer. I've only used it once. I never really had the patience or energy to cook, although there was a period where I tried, but that attempt at a lifestyle change didn't last long.

Eventually, I concluded that what *happened,* happened, and it was pure. In the heat of the moment. No thinking, no deliberating. If I had stopped and attempted to calm myself, I would have replenished the curse that has plagued my life. I would have to return home to the same bullshit.

Thinking about what Francis said about my mother, I'm not entirely sure if what he said was the truth. Yet, Francis was never one to have a great imagination.

So, what if my mother killed my father? If my father was anything like Francis, I salute her.

So, what if she killed herself? Guilt is a boulder on the consciousness, and most can't bear the weight.

I don't feel guilt. Not anymore.

There was no longer a disconnect between God and me. We were one in the same now. From time to time, I felt the numbness in my fingers and the tickle in my throat. To subdue the entity's rebellion, I'd take a sterile cotton tipped applicator—one of those big, long Q-Tips the doctors use—and when nobody was looking, dip it into whatever blood sample I was working with at the time and suck on it like a lollipop.

Wendy entered the lab again just as I was about to leave for the day. We danced the awkward *you-go-this-way-I-go-that-way* dance for a moment before it blurted out of me.

"Can I take you to dinner?"

"Excuse me?" Her playful smile faded. I caught her off guard. I caught myself off guard.

"You know," I ran with it, "for covering for me. Getting Geraldo off my back while I was out." I kept my face as straight as possible, but my heart was thumping against my chest. I'm surprised she couldn't hear it.

"I don't know. I—"

"Come on, I owe you one." I said. "Just dinner. Nothing crazy. It's the least I could do."

She bit her bottom lip and peered up at me with her murky ponds. It took everything I had to keep my arousal from displaying itself.

"Okay," she said. My heart somersaulted. "But I can't tonight. How does tomorrow sound?"

I cleared my throat and prayed that my voice still worked. "Awesome. Tomorrow night is perfect."

"Cool."

"Cool," I echoed. "Pick you up around eight?"

"Sounds good."

"See you then."

I side-stepped past her and fought to suppress my childish grin until I was out of her sight, but before I could get out the door...

"Don't you need my address?"

"Oops. Duh. Yeah."

"Umm..." Wendy scanned the lab, searching for something to jot it down on.

"Do you have Facebook?" I asked.

"Yeah."

"I'll just find you on there and shoot you a message."

"Oh, okay," she said. Nodding, "That works."

"Talk to you soon, Wendy."

"Have a good night, Dr. Phillips."

I left the lab, light as a feather.

I have only had intercourse with three women.

I lost my virginity to Meredith Atwell when I was fifteen. She was the older sister of my childhood friend, David. She was seven years my elder. I was having a sleepover at his house, and he fell asleep halfway through whatever shitty movie we were watching in the dark living room. His father worked nights and his mother had already been in bed for hours. In hindsight, it was obvious she was junked out on pills and wine. I didn't realize that then, however. I just figured she was always tired.

It was a little past midnight when Meredith stumbled through the front door, she walked like a sailor on a rough sea; she was as drunk as one too.

The details are fuzzy, but not long after her entrance, I found myself in her room. I sat on the edge of her bed with my shorts around my ankles. She commanded me, and I quote, to "spit on your dick."

I did.

She turned her back to me, hiked up her skirt, reached between her legs, gripped my member, and guided it into her. The warmth and the initial friction of insertion and the randomness of the whole situation had me done before she even started her aggressive bouncing.

I didn't say anything.

Minutes later, after I finished a second time, I was still rock solid. I mustered up the confidence and asked her if she wanted to change positions. She said, "No, I don't want to look at you."

It became apparent why when she licked her index and middle fingers, reached down to her loins, and manually assisted herself. As she climaxed, she moaned and continually repeated the name "Robert" until she pressed all her weight on me, dug her nails into my bent knees, and quivered with euphoria. Her inside walls squeezed me tight, and I finished for a third time.

I never found out who this *Robert* was, but apparently he was unattainable, so she used me instead, an *avatar cock*. I didn't mind.

After that night, David stopped talking to me. Somehow, I assume he found out I fucked his sister. Or rather, his sister fucked me.

The two other women, that happened during college. I was too drunk when it happened to recall any details, let alone their names. Unfortunate. Waking up naked next to two naked women with no recollection of what happened is equivalent to walking out of a theatre with an empty popcorn bag and no fucking idea of what movie you just saw.

What I'm getting at is that I was rusty. I needed some practice, to clear the proverbial cobwebs, so when my chance with Wendy arose, I wouldn't disappoint.

On my drive over, I imagined a half-assed *Pretty Woman* scenario. Pick up the prostitute, provide her with a decent wardrobe, take her out to dinner, maybe a few drinks, then go back to my place for some intimate activities. Essentially a trial run, so I could assess the mistakes I made and figure out how to fix them before the real date with Wendy.

When I pulled up to the corner, Love, which I had concluded was the leader, or at least the most assertive of the group, sauntered up to my passenger door and tapped on the window.

I rolled it down.

"Hey, Sugar," Love said, "looking for a little

action?" I ignored her and cocked my head to look past her. Snowflake was leaning against the wall, puffing on a cigarette. She wore the same outfit as last time; they all did. It was no different than the first night I encountered the squad of hookers like they reverted to default positions while awaiting the next patron.

"Snowflake," I said, trying to catch her attention. Love still leaning in my open passenger side window rolled her eyes. She stood up and turned to the rest of the girls.

"Snowflake," Love barked. "Looks like ya' got a request."

Snowflake flicked her cigarette onto the sidewalk and stepped on it before her stroll over to the window. She leaned in and, with a dry repetition of a door-to-door salesman, rattled off a list of prices. I cleared my throat and interrupted the recitation of her script.

"Do you remember me?"

She narrowed her eyes and tilted her head. Her lips were slightly parted and revealed her front teeth as she scoured her memory bank.

I brought my arm up to my face and buried my mouth in the pit of my elbow. I moved my jaw up and down and raised my eyebrows while maintaining eye contact with her.

Her parted lips evolved into a superficial smirk.

"Oh," she said, returning her head to its natural, upright position. "Hey, *you.*"

"Gary," I said.

"Whatever." The smirk disappeared. "The prices are still the same. Unfortunately for you, I don't do discounts for return customers."

"Understood," I retrieved a readied roll of bills from my jacket pocket. I held the cash up for her to see. "Business is business."

The *Pretty Woman* idea went to shit as soon as she got in the car, for no other reason than it was a stupid fucking idea to begin with. I pulled a sharp U-turn and sped off.

"Where we headed?" Snowflake lit up a cigarette.

"Home."

TEN

About two blocks from the shady corner, Snowflake was generous enough to inform me that my time had started already regardless of how far of a drive it was to my townhouse.

After about five awkward minutes of oral, I patted her on her back to let her know I've had enough; I couldn't get it up. I think it's safe to say that the church van next to us at the red light knew exactly what was going on when they witnessed Snowflake's head rise up from my lap. She squashed any doubts the people in the van may have had when she made eye contact with the driver, winked, licked her lips, and blew him a kiss.

Part of me worried that Francis would be back on his recliner watching sports and chain smoking like nothing ever happened. The anxiety was equivalent to the feeling that the stove was left on all day. I opened the front door and poked my head in; he wasn't in the living room. The relief was like that of returning to a not-burned-down house.

As soon as Snowflake and I stepped foot in my abode, Snowflake stuck her hand in her purse and rustled it around within the contents. "Hey, you got a bathroom I could use real quick?"

"Yeah," I said, and pointed to the stairs. "Upstairs, first door on the right."

I never got around to fully cleaning the bathroom. The floor was still sticky with dried piss and vomit, but at least I got the shitty clothes out of there.

"Does this count against my time?" I asked.

Snowflake was already halfway up the stairs. "I'll be quick," she said, not stopping or turning to looking at me.

I waited in the living room until I heard the bathroom door close upstairs. I made my way to Francis' room, his door was partly open. I peeked inside; he was still there, face annihilated. Not moving. I listened intently for the sound of his breath. There was none. I closed the door and sauntered upstairs.

I entered my room located down the hall,

one door past the bathroom on the left and shed my clothes. I executed a few naked poses, not sure which one I should be in when Snowflake finally finished up in the bathroom. I stood in the doorway, legs splayed and elbow up and leaning on the doorframe. She was taking forever and I started to feel like an idiot, so I skulked back to my bed and sat down on the edge. I figured it was a good a time as any to message Wendy for her address.

I did.

Ten minutes and counting, Snowflake was still in the bathroom, so I spent another few minutes attempting to fluff myself, but the simple fact that I was masturbating while a hooker—that I had already purchased—was in the other room irritated me.

Twenty minutes later. Ridiculous.

I strolled down the hall to the bathroom and knocked on the door, but there was no answer. I twisted the door handle, and it clicked. Unlocked. Slowly opening the door, I caught a glimpse of Snowflake on the toilet.

"Oh, sorry," I said, diverting my eyes.

She didn't respond.

I took another gander.

Her head hung loose on her shoulders; her jet-black hair draped down and created a veil over her face. Her body was a ragdoll, haphazardly placed on the toilet. A section of rubber hose was tied tight around her arm just a few inches above the syringe that dangled from the pit of her elbow. The needle was embedded too deep and clung to her flesh. Poor form.

I entered the bathroom, knelt, and pulled the syringe from her arm and placed it on the counter. I brushed the hair out of her face with the back of my fingers, she lifted her head and her once icy-blue eyes, now dull, found mine.

"Sorry," she slurred. "I must've nodded off." She tried to stand up but stumbled. I caught her. Her face pressed against my bare chest, and she gave my sternum a tired kiss.

"I'm not paying you for this," I said.

She melted to her knees, her face slid down my torso as she did. She grabbed my limp manhood with a loose grip and tugged it toward her slacked mouth.

I reached down, grabbed her wrist, and took a step back. "Not right here."

I stood her up; my hands placed under her armpits like one would pick up a toddler. I led her to my room, stopped at the bed, and pushed her onto it. Her knees bent over the foot of my bed, and she squirmed and smiled and attempted to pull down her skirt. I helped her.

She had an unnaturally large bust for her petite figure. The way they fought gravity was either a sign that they were fake or she had phenomenal genetics. I enjoyed them either way. Her skin was so pale that it almost glowed. She reached down across her belly with both hands, her right one found herself and her left stretched farther, grasping at the air, searching for my flaccid member just a few inches out of reach. I should have been more than ready, but I wasn't. I thought a little more foreplay might get me in the mood.

Snowflake moaned a subtle moan, but her legs remained rubbery and languished, hanging off the foot of my bed and over my shoulders. The opposite of the tentacle-like force they had the last time I was down there. To be fair, there was no blood to motivate me. I was definitely phoning it in. Still, it wasn't working for me.

My phone vibrated and rattled on the hardwood floor next to me. I came up for air and, freeing up my hands as well, snatched it up. There was a notification from Wendy; she must have responded with her address. I unlocked my phone and opened the message.

"Hey," Snowflake slurred, "why'd ya' stop?"

"Wait," I grunted.

Reading the message from Wendy sent a strange, but enjoyable, sensation in my belly. It lit the fire. I could feel the blood rushing to my loins. I clicked on Wendy's picture at the top of the message, and it led me to her profile. I started to peruse through her photo albums.

I stood up and Snowflake pressed her chin against her chest and peered at my crotch through her cleavage. "Mmm…" She hummed. "Looks like someone's ready to play."

"Shut up." I reached over and grabbed her shirt from the pile of her clothes that were strewn next to her naked body on the bed. I tossed it on her, and it landed on her throat. "Put that over your face."

"Huh?"

"Put that shirt over your fucking face."

"Okay." She complied. "Kinky," she followed up, her voice muffled through the cheap polyester blouse.

"And don't talk."

Snowflake raised her hand and gave a thumbs

up.

I opened the "*Beach Time!!!*" photo album and placed my phone on Snowflake's tight stomach, right below her belly button.

I periodically swiped through the photos as I thrusted. I savored it, slowed down, and held off a little longer. A few times Snowflake would mutter something and I'd kindly remind her to shut the fuck up.

When it was time, when I felt the surge of euphoria about to course through me, I found myself staring at the seventh photo in the album. Wendy wore a white bikini; the water must've been cold that day. My eyes darted from her murky ponds to her breasts, to her bikini bottoms and back, and I stammered a slew of unintelligible words out loud that I don't recall.

When it finally came, the sensation was so strong that my legs became useless. I sank forward onto Snowflake; her body was cool against mine, like the underside of a pillow in the middle of a summer night. Panting heavily as if I had just finished a triathlon, I rolled off Snowflake and onto my back next to her. She peeled the shirt off her face and cocked her head to face me.

"Who's Wendy?" she asked.

I ignored her.

My heartbeat synced up with the creak of the ceiling fan, my mind mesmerized by its gyration and everything else had begun to fade away.

I felt warm in a frigid world, so I closed my eyes.

ELEVEN

The scream woke me.

The echo bounced through the hall and resonated in the room. My eyes opened wide, my body was heavy. I reached out to my left and felt nothing but the indentation in the mattress where Snowflake used to be.

I sat up and, with my head on a swivel, scanned the room. Her clothes that were strewn across the bed earlier were gone too. I sprung to my feet, my posture stiff as a *T-1000*. I didn't bother getting dressed before I sprinted out the door and down the stairs.

Snowflake was exiting Francis' room when I reached the bottom floor. Her eyes were practically lidless when she saw me. She froze and dropped her purse. An unopened pack of Francis' Lucky Strikes, a few pill bottles with his name on them, and a couple of knick-knacks I had then realized were missing off my shelves had spilled out onto the floor along with a few items of her own.

"I..." *It's not what it looks like*, I finished my sentence in my head.

No, it's exactly what it looks like: An old man with his face bashed in was in that room, rotting.

"I have to go," Snowflake said in a shivering whisper. "I have to go." Her voice returned and calmer this time around.

She kneeled and scooped up her purse, neglecting the items that had spilled out. She took one quick glance at me still perched at the bottom of the stairway. In a hurried stroll, almost a frantic skip, she made way for the front door.

I did too.

My strides were mechanical in nature. The exact moment her fingertips met the doorknob, I reached out and found a handful of her hair.

She arched her back and yelped. She dropped her purse again and both her hands reached up and clasped onto my forearm.

I pulled her back across my body like I was yanking the ripcord on a stubborn lawnmower.

She left her feet and her back made a raw slapping sound as she hit hardwood floor.

She writhed and winced and coughed. She rolled onto her side, clutched her stomach, brought her knees to her chest, and started to cry.

I locked the deadbolt on the front door before dragging Francis' vacant, haggard recliner toward it. I slammed the old, smelly thing against the door, creating an impromptu blockade.

Snowflake was still on the floor, unable to catch her breath. I used the opportunity to quickly scour the garage, grabbing whatever I could: a segment of neon-yellow rope, four bungee cords, a couple rolls of duct tape, and a big, blue, plastic tarp. The shit Francis had, but never fucking used. He was a utility store junkie and always preached about being ready for *when everything went to shit*. Well, I'd considered this *shit*. Just not the kind either Francis or I had the foresight to see. Nonetheless, it happened that Francis' anything-but-frugal spending was useful for something.

I threw everything in the tarp, brought the corners together creating a makeshift sack, and slung it over my shoulder. On my way out of the garage, I lurked into the small galley kitchen and snatched a filet knife that hung from one of those fancy magnetic strips on the wall; another loaded purchase from my "cooking" phase.

When I returned to Snowflake, she was sitting up and collecting herself. Her tears left her thick, black mascara bedraggled and created streams of gray lines on her pale cheeks like cracks on concrete. Her ruby lipstick remained perfect. Not smeared at all, even from the escapades earlier. I liked it more than the black lipstick she wore during our first encounter.

"Get up," I said.

"Please," she said, swallowing the lump in her throat. "Please, Gary. Please. Let me leave."

I pointed the knife at her. "Get up."

As if I flipped on a faucet, another deluge of tears poured down her face. Reluctant, she rose to her feet, her posture hunched as she held her open palm against her sternum.

"Please," she sobbed. "I'm sorry. I shouldn't have stolen. I—"

"Go." I said. I lifted my chin and motioned to Francis' room.

She shook her head while remaining eye contact with me, her lower lip riddled with tremors. "Plea—"

"Go."

Snowflake didn't put up a fight.

I had her crawl into Francis' bed beside his corpse. I draped the plastic tarp over their bodies like a comforter. Then, I tucked the loose ends of the tarp under the mattress at their feet and sides, only leaving their heads exposed. Pulling it tight, leaving no slack. I stretched the bungee cords from one side of the bed, over their bodies, to the other, hooking them to the underside of the bedframe. One across the chest, one across the belly, one across the thighs, and one just above the ankles. Using the rolls of duct tape, I patterned a few layers over and between the bungee cords for reinforcement. From the segment of neon rope, I then made a half-assed noose and fastened it around Snowflake's neck.

She wept.

Something about that made her more attractive.

It made her human. No longer just an object. She felt *things*.

Like fear, and sorrow.

Her eyes watched me as I worked. I was her world, only I mattered now.

I was *God*.

I wrapped the loose end of the rope to the bedpost in a makeshift pulley system and tugged.

Snowflake's chin hiked up toward the ceiling. Her neck stretched and strained, and I could see the jugular veins and carotid arteries pulsate along the sides of her throat.

"Plea—" Snowflake groaned and struggled to cough. "Please," she croaked.

I stood at her side, nude, legs spread, hands on my hips, chest out, and hard as steel like Superman with an overactive libido. I scanned the bed up and down, double-checking my work. I brought my face down and halted a few inches from Snowflake's. "I'll be right back," I whispered. Strolling to the door and, without looking back, I said, "Don't go anywhere."

I chuckled the whole way to the upstairs bathroom and back. I retrieved the syringe and rubber hose that sat on the bathroom counter. When I returned, I sat on the floor next to Snowflake and started tinkering.

Diligently, I removed the plunger from the syringe, leaving me with an open-ended barrel and needle. I finagled one end of the rubber hose to the open end and wrapped the last strip of duct tape around the seam where the hose and barrel were conjoined. I smoothed out the tape and made sure the joint was airtight.

I stuck the other end of the rubber hose in the side of my mouth like a piece of licorice, pressed my lips tight, and sucked. It wasn't the best flow, but it would do.

Gently, I bit down on the hose as it hung from my mouth like a loose cigarette. I leaned in and kissed Snowflake's strained, elongated throat. I then whispered in her ear, "You're gonna feel a little prick." I took the needle and slowly, meticulously, but excitedly, slid it into her carotid artery. The pop of flesh as the needle penetrated stole my breath like the first steep drop of a rollercoaster ride.

Snowflake struggled to struggle, but no more than an uncomfortable wiggle was feasible.

I sucked softly at first, letting the natural pumping of her blood gradually saturate the barrel. Steadily, I increased the intensity of my suction. Her blood left the translucent, tan rubber hose black as it crawled toward my salivating mouth.

Realizing it would be easier if I let gravity lend a helping hand, I sat down on the floor and leaned my back against the bed. The rubber hose stretched a little, but the flow was much more efficient. I consumed and consumed and, like a drunk wearing one of those beer hats, consumed some more. Every time Snowflake moaned or cried or struggled to move, I sucked harder.

It could have been twenty minutes.

It could have been two hours.

However long I was siphoning blood from Snowflake's body, she had become silent and still a little after halfway through the process.

I peeled the rubber hose from my mouth. Blood had coated my lips and my chin and had partly dried to a sticky substance. My belly bulged like a starving Ethiopian child. Yet, I was full.

I moseyed to my feet and inspected Snowflake; her head twisted upward, her neck stretched, her eyes open, but lost. Her mouth slightly agape. There was some red, raw skin from the rope's friction, and some bruising around the needle. I pulled it out and ran my fingers along her throat. She was cold. Colder than usual and her flesh took on a bluish hue. Her life force now ran through me.

Fueled me.

Satisfied me.

The most important thing she had ever done in her life was giving it to me.

Power. She relinquished hers to give me more.

Snowflake The Sacrifice.

I freed her neck from the noose and her head

went limp.

"Thank you," I whispered to her lifeless face before kissing her passionately on her idle lips. I closed the door on the way out and went back upstairs to bed.

TWELVE

To say I was a god wasn't hyperbolic unless the one who claimed so subscribed to the idea of a god being perfect in every way. Physically, emotionally, intellectually, and spiritually. Absolutely flawless. Those ideologies, those beliefs, however, are steamy loads of utter bullshit.

The Greeks, Egyptians, Babylonians, and Sumerians, I believe, had the proper take on the matter. Their gods had flaws. Their gods had interpersonal beefs, drama, and relations. They fought each other, they fucked each other, they killed each other. Like Zeus' insatiable lust for everything—even animals—or Ishtar's relentless conquest for power and devious methods of seduction... I too, had an Achilles' Heel.

Wendy Carter.

My yearning for her left me powerless. She was my mountain to climb; her love and embrace would be my prize to claim. She was a Goddess Queen, and I was ready to win her over, join her side, and be her God King.

I debated calling the hospital to let them know I wasn't going to come in today. I ran through my excuses: I still didn't feel well, or my grandfather had fallen ill. I decided not to call at all. Fuck 'em.

I arrived at Wendy's house almost an hour early. I figured I'd park a couple of doors down and out of view of her windows. The last thing I wanted was to look too eager—or creepy.

The first snow of the season fell from the icy clouds, peppering the asphalt with the tiny white flakes. It didn't take long, but they started to accumulate faster than they melted. Soon, Claybrook City would be covered in a blanket of white, giving its denizens a subtle contrast within the drab gray construction of their city.

With that said, Wendy lived in a quaint little neighborhood just outside of the inner city. Unlike the plain concrete structures that I've become so accustomed to downtown, all the houses were painted with pastel greens, blues, and pinks. Their white trimming matched the small, white, uniformed picket fences that wrapped around their tiny front yards. Although, at first glance, the houses seemed unique in aesthetic, every other aspect of them could be defined as "cookie cutter." The designers really went out on a limb to give them some color—especially for Claybrook City.

I didn't like it.

It was five minutes until I had to pick up Wendy. Anxious, my hands shook. I held onto the steering wheel with an attempt to settle them but just ended up white knuckling so hard that my palms began to ache; the blisters were just beginning to heal.

Four minutes.

I clenched my jaw and, regardless of how cold it was outside, I rolled down the windows and took off my jacket. I was sweating profusely.

Three minutes.

I used every scrap of paper trash I could find in the backseat of my car and attempted to wipe the sweat from my face, neck, and armpits. Newspapers, junk mail, and loose napkins from fast food joints.

Two minutes.

I slid back into my jacket, but I left the windows down. I adjusted my rearview mirror and fixed my hair, I think I had become balder over the last few days. Either that, or my nerves were fucking with me.

One minute.

I thought about bailing out. I ran through a half-dozen excuses and justifications in my mind but ultimately manned up. This could be my only chance.

I pulled up to the front of Wendy's house about five minutes late. I retrieved my phone from my jacket pocket and messaged her, "Out front. Sorry I'm late. Started snowing and traffic got crazy."

Awaiting the response felt like an eternity, I stared at the screen without blinking. Finally, three dots appeared. Then they disappeared. Then they appeared again followed by, "Okay. I'll just be a few minutes."

I sat in silence. It didn't bother me none, but realizing this, I thought Wendy would think it was weird, so I switched on the radio. Station after station belched out Christmas tunes and the various rehashings of them. I remembered why I left the fucking thing off this time of year.

Somewhere in the AM frequency, I found a channel that wasn't so festive. It was a classical music station, complete with the soft, pretentious voiced disc jockey. I had no idea what song was playing, let alone what key they were playing in. I didn't give a shit either way. However, I thought that Wendy would think that I was distinguished. So, I left it on.

When Wendy finally exited her house, time slowed as she made her way down the cheap, cobblestone pathway littered with fresh snow. She was absolutely stunning. I've never seen her not in scrubs, apart from the pictures in her various social media photo albums.

Photos did no justice, however.

She wore a forest green dress that flowed and halted just above her knees. Her black leggings matched her black pea coat. The way the bright, white snow kissed her coat and juxtaposed with the black felt material, I may as well have been watching a cinematic masterpiece. She wore boots that rose just above her ankles, and they had a little tuft of black fur around the cuff. Subtly, not the dramatic, Eskimo-style boots that were trendy a few years back. Damn, those were gaudy. If you ever wanted to know what kind of girl to avoid, just look at her footwear during the winter months.

I was more drawn to Wendy than ever and

found myself leaning over the passenger seat to get a better look at her as she approached. Our eyes met and I played off my strange position by opening the passenger door and pushing it open.

"Thank you." She smiled as she climbed in. She closed the door and instantly put on her seatbelt.

I had to force myself to break my gaze. I tried my best, but I kept finding my eyes back on her.

DJ Robert S. Bobowitz dampened the long, awkward silence between us with his soothing voice. I snapped out of it when the choir of violins and violas assaulted my ears. "Where do you want to eat?"

"I thought you had that figured out."

Shit.

"I, uh..." My lips were dry and cracked. I licked them. It stung. "I have a few ideas. Just figured I'd ask you what you're in the mood for. If you have any preference, ya know?"

"Not really," she said. "Whatever is fine with me."

"Alright then." I put the car in drive. "Off we go."

I guess I was so consumed with the fact that Wendy agreed to go out with me that I let the actual planning of the event slip through the cracks, so I just drove with no real destination in mind but kept my eyes open for a nice place we could sit and chat.

Blah Blah No. 5 in the key of *who gives a shit* was playing and the use of timpani and crashes were making my skin crawl.

"Feel free to change the station to whatever," I said, masking the irritability and eagerness for her to do so in my voice.

"You sure?"

"Yeah," I said, before I proceeded to lie, "I've heard this one a billion times."

Wendy leaned forward and flipped through the stations before stopping on one that was playing Frank Sinatra's rendition of "White Christmas".

"Oh, I love this song," Wendy said.

"Me too!" Fuck me. "It's a classic!"

Sometime after Celine Dion's take on "O Holy Night" and halfway through some horrid pop-rock version of "The Little Drummer Boy", I spotted a stand-alone restaurant on the corner of wherever we were. It was called *Raphael's Steakhouse.*

"Hey," I said, "this place alright with you?" I pointed at it as I merged into the turning lane.

"Sure."

Wendy and I walked into the almost empty restaurant. We were instantly seated, then instantly greeted by our server, a young man with a plastic smile and perfect posture.

I ordered the house steak—rare—and Wendy ordered the tilapia with a side garden salad.

The next ten minutes consisted of me fidgeting in my chair because those fucking Christmas songs were present—they really were inescapable—and Wendy kept her face buried in her phone.

"So..." I mustered up the balls to say something. "How are things?"

"Good," she said, looking up for a brief second and smiling before returning her focus back to the timewaster in her hand.

"Good," I echoed.

What the hell was taking so long?

Other than us, there were maybe two other people in the dining room. It shouldn't take that long to prepare a rare steak and slab of fish.

When the waiter eventually returned, he placed our meals in front of us and only then did Wendy slide her phone back into her purse that sat on the floor next to her chair. She unrolled the cloth napkin and retrieved her silverware and I did the same.

"This looks yummy," she said.

"Indeed, it does." I stopped the waiter before he left, "Can we get some *drinks*?"

"Of course, Sir. I have a wonderful merlot that pairs well with the steak." He turned to Wendy, "And a nice, crisp chardonnay that would enhance your dining experience with that tilapia."

Jesus Christ, kid. The place was a hole-in-the-wall steakhouse, but he made it feel like a five-star restaurant.

"Ooh." Wendy's eyes widened. That was a good sign.

"That sounds great," I said. "If you see an empty glass, don't hesitate to bring us a fresh one."

"Of course, Sir." The waiter said before he strutted through the swinging double doors and into the kitchen.

Wendy and I didn't speak while we ate. Instead, the endless stream of festive music and the clinks and clanks of metal forks and knives scraping against porcelain plates raped my eardrums. I wasn't hungry, but Wendy didn't notice I was mostly cutting my steak up into tiny pieces rather than eating it.

Somewhere around Wendy's third or fourth glass of white wine, she started to open up. Unprovoked. She told me about her older brother's start up business, a mobile pet euthanasia service. She told me about her younger sister and how she just got accepted into an Ivy League school. She described to me a funny scene in a romantic comedy she watched on television the other night.

And I just listened.

Wendy revealed things to me that I already knew from my constant visitation of her profiles on social media, but I feigned surprised and intrigue until I wasn't feigning anymore. Something about her actually telling me made them more real than they ever were. Like how she had a pug named Ninja and a golden retriever named Vlad. Or how much she loved visiting the ocean because the vastness of it made her worries feel small and unimportant and at first, it made her feel insecure, but now she appreciated the positive perspective it gives her.

Wendy told me things I didn't know, too. She told me that she dated her ex-boyfriend, Tim, from freshman year in high school up to the time she enrolled in college to become a phlebotomist. She caught him cheating and it sent her into depression. One day, something clicked, and she left him and enrolled in college in a desperate attempt to change her lifestyle and get her shit together. She said it worked out for the most part.

Wendy's tone went from giddy to somber to giddy as she steamrolled me with blurbs and snippets about her life. The fact that she did was a sign of comfort.

I enjoyed that.

I enjoyed it so much I even felt the urge to hum along with the Christmas tunes that serenaded us in the dimly lit dining room of *Raphael's Steakhouse*.

I loved her.

The more details she unveiled about her life, I loved her more and more.

I thought I loved her from the first moment she walked into the lab as an intern a few years ago, but I see now that was just a lustful limerence. The more she spoke and the longer she gazed at me with those murky ponds of hers, the more infatuated I had become. I didn't know it was possible, but I fell deeper and deeper into the well of love and I didn't think I'd ever hit the bottom. The more I fell, the more vulnerable I felt.

Wendy's phone chimed, interrupting her story about how good she used to be at volleyball in high school. She leaned over and dug it out of her purse. She glanced at whatever notification popped up on her home screen, smiled, and then placed it face down on the table.

"Well, this was fun," she said. "Sorry about my babbling."

"No, no, don't be sorry. I enjoyed getting to know you more. You've led an interesting life and have a unique perspective on things."

"*Sure*," she giggled sarcastically.

I winked and knocked back the remaining merlot in my glass. I was about to flag down our waiter for another until Wendy stood up.

"It's getting late," she said as she removed her pea coat that hung on the back of her chair and slid it on. "I have the early shift tomorrow," she said with a playful frown.

Betrayed by time, I nodded in agreement and stood.

"Mind giving me a ride home?"

"Well, I drove you here. Not gonna make you take a taxi."

"You've had about a whole bottle of wine, that's why I ask," she said. "You good to drive?"

"I'm fine." I smiled, tossing a hundred-dollar bill on the table. "More than good. Great."

It had not stopped snowing while we were inside the steakhouse. The roads and sidewalks were blanketed with white under the dark, cloudy night sky. Surely the roads would be plowed and salted by morning, but until then, it forced me to drive slowly.

Traffic was tedious to say the least. Any other day this hindrance would be a thorn in my side, but that night Wendy was in the car, singing softly along with the Christmas tunes. At that moment, I prayed for an avalanche; an avalanche would force us to be trapped together. I wished for anything and everything to make that night with her last longer.

I knew exactly how to get back to her house but pretended to get lost and wander aimlessly around her neighborhood. Wendy, as helpful as always, punched her address into the GPS on her phone and dictated the directions to me.

That squashed that plan.

When we pulled up to her house, she turned to face me, thanked me for dinner, smiled, turned back and proceeded to open the door. But before she pushed it open, I reached out and placed my open hand on her inner thigh. The warmth that emanated from her groin thawed my icy soul and sent a jolt of excitability and blood rushing into my loins.

"Hey," I whispered.

Wendy turned to face me again. Startled, she glanced down at my hand that had crept a few more inches up her dress.

That's when I leaned in and kissed her. For those few seconds, her soft, luscious lips were soothing against my chapped ones. My fingertips grazed her other pair of lips through her leggings. They were just as soft, but more luscious.

In one swift movement, she moaned a disapproving moan, grabbed my wrist, lifted it away from her lap, and jerked her face away from mine, peeling our lips apart. "Whoa."

"What?"

"Dr. Phillips, I—"

"Gary."

"Gary..."

"Yes, Wendy?" My hand hovered over her hiked skirt and itched to caress her.

"Gary, I'm sorry, but I'm not attracted to you in that way."

My waning hand evolved into a fist, and I reigned it in and returned it to my side. My chest deflated.

"You're a nice guy and all…" Wendy searched for the words. "But you're not my type. Plus, I just started seeing someone and I don't want to make things complicated."

I remained silent, pursing my cracked lips and glaring at her nervous face.

"Okay, well, have a good night, Gary." She opened the door and climbed out. "Thanks again."

Wendy closed the door and scooted her feet through the now six inches of snow that obscured her walkway before disappearing through her front door.

I drove around the block and parked where I had parked earlier. A few houses down from hers, I turned off the engine and switched off the headlights. I changed the radio station back to classical and I waited. I wasn't sure what for, but I wasn't ready to leave just yet.

I waited for over an hour; my gaze locked on Wendy's house down the street.

Halfway through "Winter", the first movement in Antonio Vivaldi's "The Four Seasons" in G-minor, a slick car, I believe it was a newer model Audi, pulled up and parked in front of Wendy's house. It was too dark to see who exited the car, but they were carrying something and headed straight to the door.

I thought maybe it was a pizza delivery guy, but the fact that the car was so nice, it was kind of late, and Wendy didn't strike me as the type of girl to eat dinner twice, I knew something was off. When the mysterious driver didn't return to the vehicle after another ten minutes of waiting, I absolutely knew something wasn't right.

I got out of my car and trudged along the snowy sidewalk. Once I approached Wendy's house, I kept my head low so as to not be seen. I worked my way over her picket fence that peaked a little short of my crotch. There was a big window that faced the street just above two patches of shrubbery. I snuck over and squatted between them. Curtains veiled the inside, but they weren't completely drawn closed.

A fissure, a rift.

Light oozed through the seam, allowing me to see inside. Diligently, I raised my head just above the base of the window and peered in.

It took everything I had not to break the glass. A lifetime of patience and turning the other cheek couldn't prepare me for this. My body burned and I swore the snow had melted around my feet. I was peeping into Wendy's living room. A bouquet of flowers—Yellow Geminis—and a box of chocolates sat on the coffee table. Wendy, who had changed into a loose, cotton, sleeveless blue blouse and a pair of comfy-looking, pink pajama pants with cartoonish graphics of dog bones and puppies on them, sat on the couch with her legs spread wide. A man leaned over her; the back of his head faced me. The curtains obscured most of his body, but I could see his hand was shoved down the front of Wendy's pants and visibly making a circular motion.

Wendy bit her lip like she does. Her eyes were closed and her head craned back. One of her hands clawed at the man's back while the other vigorously rubbed his crotch through his slacks.

Wendy whispered something in his ear, and he removed his hand from inside her. He stood up, faced Wendy still seated on the couch, his back still toward me. She removed her shirt. Her breasts were no bigger than my palm and her nipples were only a few shades darker pink than the rest of her flesh.

Divine.

Flawless.

Perfect.

I pulled out my member the same time the faceless man dropped trough. I swiped the tears and snot from my face with my sleeve. The cold air stung my exposed self that I gripped a little too tight in my hand.

Wendy and the man were positioned at just the right angle for me to see her perform. She kissed and licked and devoured him with such passion, with such ambition; like it was the best thing she had ever tasted. All while looking up at the man with her murky ponds and retaining eye contact.

Now, with both my hands below, I tried to emulate the pace and motion of Wendy's mouth and hands in real time. Periodically, my vision blurred and I'd have to pause and wipe the freezing tears from my eyes. The familiar rise of euphoria started to build up and pressurize, but it did not feel good this time. It was a painful, grueling experience. Not unlike the pain of trying to pop a pimple that is not ready to pop with the hope that you'll get that well-worth-it, gratifying release.

A few more seconds and I would have gotten that release. But they stopped. Wendy removed the man from her mouth, peered up at him and smiled before she said something I couldn't hear.

He nodded.

Wendy stood up, removed her pajama bottoms, propped up on her toes, and kissed the man. Her naked body was better than I had ever imagined.

I squeezed myself tight and felt my racing pulse resonate through my calloused palm. A drizzle of warm prerelease oozed over my knuckles as I awaited the next act.

Wendy turned around and presented herself to him like something out of a wildlife documentary. He reached around and groped her breasts and pressed himself against her exposed backside. It was when she pulled away, took his hand, and started to lead him somewhere I couldn't see is when I caught a glimpse of who the man was.

I let go of myself and, I must have been holding my breath, because I gasped for air like I'd just surfaced after ascending from the bottom of the ocean.

That man was Dr. Lucas Geraldo.

THIRTEEN

This was the end.

I was powerless.

I fled the scene. I deliberated smashing the rear window of Geraldo's luxury vehicle with a fist-sized stone but decided I didn't want to draw any unwanted attention. I don't recall much about the drive home except for a brass-heavy composition blaring through the speakers. When I pulled into my driveway, I turned off the engine and the radio and thought about how I'd do it in silence.

Hanging?

No. That wasn't *my* style.

Overdose on a cocktail of pills?

No. Too slow. Too poetic.

Hook a hose up to the exhaust of my car and hotbox myself? No. First, I drive a fucking hybrid, and the set-up would be an endeavor in itself.

A Bullet to the head?

Yeah, that works.

Francis kept his standard issue M1911 semi-automatic pistol in a lockbox under his bed with other relics from his service in Vietnam. The only reason I know what kind of fucking gun it was is because I've been forced to listen to his bullshit war stories every other day my entire life.

That was it. That was how it would end. I wonder how long I'd be rotting before anyone cared to look. Shit, I'd be halfway to a petrified skeleton before someone asked, *"Where's Gary?"*

I entered through the front door of my townhouse. The living room was still a mess from my fiasco with Snowflake. The recliner was tipped on its side and only moved enough away from the door so it could open. I propped it up and put it back where it's been for so many years prior. I figured I'd do it there, on the recliner.

I was heading toward the kitchen to grab a beer—my last beer—before I blew my brains out, and that's when I heard the talking.

"There he goes again," a grizzled voice said. "Just gonna crawl back in his fuckin' hole."

"Looks like it," a high-pitched voice agreed. "Except this time he won't be able to climb out of it." The voice giggled.

"Ain't that the fuckin' truth. Good g'damn riddance." The grizzled voice joined the other with a chuckle of their own.

The voices came from Francis' room. His door was closed, so I tiptoed toward it, but froze when I heard them continue.

"It could be something to do with his baldness," the high-pitched voice said. "Or maybe his small dick."

"Ha!" The grizzled voice barked. "Is it really that small?"

"Not the smallest, but it's fucking tiny. I'd want to kill myself too."

"Ha!" The grizzled voice barked again, but louder this time. "Well, he didn't get it from my side of the family."

The talking stopped.

I took a deep breath and continued toward the door. I reached the door and idled and listened.

Nothing.

My heart rate slowed and I convinced myself I was just hearing things. Until...

"Shh," The high voice hissed. "I think he is home."

"So what?" The grizzled voice grunted. "Fuck

him!"

I felt as though the world teetered from side to side beneath my feet until I realized my head had been swaying back and forth. I leaned against Francis' closed door to regain my balance.

"Gary!" The grizzled voice boomed. "Get the fuck in here!"

My shaky hand struggled to grip the doorknob. When I was able to, I opened it a few inches and peeked in. It was too dark to see anything.

"Don't be shy, Gary," the high voice said.

I opened the door all the way and the light from the living room spilled in. Francis and Snowflake sat side by side on the edge of the bed, facing me. The beam of light cast a spotlight on them and my shadow stretched across the floorboards beneath the three feet dangling from the edge of the bed. The rest of the room was obscured by impenetrable darkness.

Snowflake's eyes were no longer the bright, icy blue, but rather black obsidian. Her flesh was ghost-white, almost translucent, with the exception of the raw, bruised ring around her throat; her black veins and arteries spider-webbed under her skin.

She smiled a sinister smile, "Hi, Gary."

Francis no longer had eyes or a nose. His face was a cavity of rot. His upper lip was swollen, his teeth broken, and his lower jaw fraught with lesions and infection. It was the only thing that moved when he spoke.

"So, are ya gonna do it, pussy?"

"Do what?" I muttered. I blinked in rapid succession; certain my eyes have deceived me.

They didn't.

"Take control, Gary." Snowflake said.

"Ya just gonna let it end like this?" Francis asked.

"What are you—"

"The gun, Gary!" Francis' jaw snapped. "Ya just gonna deep throat the barrel 'til it blows its fuckin' load in your skull? Or are ya gonna be a fuckin' man for once in your fuckin' pathetic life and take control?"

"I—"

"There's this fuckin' guy, your boss, right?" Francis continued, "He's fuckin' your broad after you wined 'n' dined her."

"Yeah, Gary," Snowflake chimed in. "She took from you, everyone took from you, and you've never received anything in return."

"Your boss is bad blood, Gary," said Francis.

"Take what you deserve. No one is going to give it to you," said Snowflake.

"Bad blood, Gary."

"Take it, like you took mine. Isn't that what you practiced for? Isn't that why I'm here, right now, still? Did I not fulfill my purpose?"

"Ya know where the gun is, Gary," Francis said. "Take it. I hope you do what ya needa do."

Their heads fell limp simultaneously. Their bodies contorted and twisted and, like a pair of worms, slithered back into the bed still blanketed with the taut, blue tarp. They went completely still.

My fingers went numb and my vision blurred. I descended to my knees and crawled toward the bed. I reached under and pulled the lockbox from obscurity. It was unlocked. I opened it and snatched the pistol. I checked the clip. It was loaded. I stood up and shoved it in my waistband before I floated upstairs.

I retrieved the box of my parents' relics and dumped it on my bed. I grabbed the keys to the house I inherited and shoved them in my pocket. When I did, I left my body.

I was mistaken. I was far too weak. I did not transmute or evolve with or into a god. Not yet. Rather, the entity let me believe I did. I tried to build a bridge and become one with the divine, but I had failed. Now it was time for them to take the wheel and course correct.

I watched my body strut into the bathroom. I then found myself within the mirror, observing my body play host to God, who in turn, observed their reflection in me. It used my mouth to speak, but the voice was not mine.

It shrilled, *"Let's go home."*

My body walked out. I was trapped in the mirror, peering out into the vacant room. The urge to scream washed over me, but before I managed to do so, I blacked out.

I flashed in and out, images of streetlights and snow flickered like an erratic slideshow. The sound of the city hummed around me; segments of Christmas tunes faded in and out.

There were stagnant moments when time didn't seem to progress and moments where I felt like I was traveling at lightspeed.

I sat hostage and caught myself looking at myself in the rearview mirror. My hand, but not my command, reached up and ripped it from the ceiling.

It's up...

To you...

There I stood, at the foot of Wendy's queen-sized bed. The room was warm and the sunflower-yellow that the walls were painted only added to the mood.

Wendy switched on the lamp on her nightstand. Everything in her room matched—the nightstand, her bed frame, the dresser tucked in the corner. The room was the definition of tidy. Even the white carpets were spotless, apart from my muddy footprints that led me here and the growing pool of blood that leaked from Ninja and Vlad's lifeless, canine bodies at my feet.

The smell of gunpowder swirled up my nostrils and tickled my sinuses.

"Gary, please," Wendy shrieked.

My right hand held the pistol pointed at Geraldo. He sat up against the headboard, hands raised to his side, frozen.

My left hand vigorously scratched an insatiable itch on the side of my head, leaving bits of bloody flakes and hair underneath my fingernails.

"Talk to me, Gary," Geraldo said. His tone was cool and collected like a well-versed detective during a hostage situation.

"No." My voice was as monotone as a robotic answering machine.

"Is it about work? I know you've been a little stressed lately. I haven't been easy on you, and I'm sorry. We are all stressed, Gary. Let's just take a minute and—"

I unloaded six shots at him. Four of them hit: two in the chest, one in the throat, and one in the belly. The other two made decent sized holes in the headboard above his right shoulder.

Geraldo slouched over to his left and his head landed in Wendy's lap. There was only a sprinkle of blood on her cheek. However, Geraldo gurgled up more blood that left a Frisbee-sized stain on the only article of clothing she wore: an oversized, white t-shirt.

She screamed.

I shot the lamp, it shattered.

The world went dark.

In and out.

Between this and nothing. I was a passenger both in life and during the drive. My hands, that I did not control, clutched the steering wheel as I watched the cityscape fade away in the side mirror.

There were trees. They were powdered with snow.

There was banging and moaning coming from inside the trunk.

Sorrow buried itself deep and I wanted to pull over, yet God focused on the road that serpentined through the forest.

There was nothing I could do.

There I was.

On the floor, I sat against the base of the loveseat between two sets of legs belonging to giants. I was two years old. We were at the house where my parents died; the house I owned but Francis refused to live in.

The living room was stuck in time. The furniture, the décor, the television in the corner was a big box with a series of dials. It was dark, only the moonlight pouring through the big, bay window allowed the scene to be visible, albeit through a soft, blue glow dominated it.

I peered up at the giant to my right. It was my father. He kept his focus directly in front of him.

"Daddy?" I beckoned. The word rippled through the ether.

I felt a warm, firm hand squeeze my left

shoulder. Like moving underwater, I turned my head to the giant on my left.

It was my mother staring down at me. She smiled.

"Gary, honey," she said. Her voice pulsated and echoed like a warped vinyl record. "You're doing such a good job!"

"Pay attention, boy." My father's voice was rolling thunder. He placed his giant, cold hand atop my head and forced me to look forward. "We can't let any mistakes happen."

As a family, we watched as I, or the entity that controlled my older body, meticulously duct taped Wendy to an old rocking chair. Her wrists were already constrained to the arms of the chair and now it worked on securing her ankles to the bowed base on either side. It was a rickety old thing. It was a rickety old thing back then, too.

Wendy jerked and attempted to rock the chair over, but its backside was pushed and propped against the wall and prohibited much movement.

I watched as Big Gary left the room. Only gone briefly, he returned with the same homemade apparatus used on Snowflake. Big Gary held the needle in his boney fingers and prepared Wendy's throat for insertion.

I flinched and my eye twitched. In my prepubescent, squeaky voice, I told Big Gary, "Her neck too pretty. Not the neck." As I said the words, so did Big Gary—verbatim—to Wendy.

Her eyes widened even more and a whole new wave of tears fell from them.

Big Gary descended to his knees, his head between Wendy's spread legs. He caressed her inner right thigh with two fingers. He found what he wanted and pushed the dull needled into her femoral artery located roughly six inches south of her tainted loins.

Big Gary sat cross-legged on the floor, between Wendy's spread legs, and started to suck from the open end of the rubber hose. The residue from Snowflake had congealed inside and made it difficult at first, but Big Gary persevered.

Wendy tried to scream, but the lower half of her face, just below her nose, was wrapped with four layers of duct tape.

As the blood crept down the hose toward Big Gary's pursed lips, Wendy violently fidgeted making the old chair creak and crack and moan, and the sudden pang of starvation hit my tiny body.

I started to cry.

"Will you shut him up?" My father roared behind me.

"Gary..."

I turned and looked up longingly at my mother. She was exhausted,

"Are you hungry?"

My colossal mother cradled me in her arms; her warm breast in my mouth, nurturing me. She gently rocked back and forth, the creaking and the cracking and the moaning of the chair like a metronome as she hummed "Rockabye Baby". She looked forward, not at me, but at something else or nothing at all, with a thousand-yard stare.

Did she forget about me?

Does she still love me?

Why won't she look at me?

I bit down on her tit and sucked harder to get her attention.

She glared down at me with her big green eyes, winced, and slid her lower lip under her front teeth. She kept biting her lip as long as I kept my sharp, little teeth latched on her nipple.

But, before long, after I was assured I had her attention, I'd release and continue my soft suckling. My eyelids grew heavy and that's when

I remembered...

I remembered what love and happiness and worth felt like. For years, all my years, I thought I had never experienced it.

I did then.

I did now.

And after I'd finished feeding, I'd never experience it again.

I made a mistake.

I wasn't watching.

Father was disappointed with me.

I was given my body back just a moment before Wendy's heel struck me in the jaw that was clamped around the rubber hose. As I flung backward, the rubber hose stretched, and like a slingshot, the needle was yanked out of Wendy's leg and shot over my head and my back flattened on the floor.

Wendy had wiggled her ankles loose from the chair while I was feeding because I had failed to supervise Big Gary.

Even gods have flaws.

She stood; her wrists still taped to the arms. She slammed the chair up and down beneath her as she tried to jerk them free.

I laid there...

In a daze, I watched her through cracked eyelids. Lethargic and tired, my tongue felt like it was too big for my mouth, my front teeth were chipped and broken, and my lower jaw had become unhinged. Blood leaked from my nostrils, gums, and split lip. I wanted nothing more than to sleep, but I knew I had to end it.

End it and I could finally rest.

As soon as I sat up, Wendy twirled, swung around, and the side of my head was met with the bottom of the rocking chair. For a few seconds, my world was only blackness, but I heard the banging of the chair on the archway into the living room constructed of thick wooden beams. The same kind that stretches from wall to wall in the exposed ceiling. The same kind of wooden beams my mother hung herself from. I heard the rambunctious cracking and creaking and finally, snapping.

When I regained some vision, I struggled to my feet. I locked eyes with Wendy as she continued to bang the chair harder against the archway. The lower half lay on the floor in a heap of splintered wood, but she was still attached to the seat and armrests. It was hiked up against her back like a mangled turtle shell. She had started to throw herself back against the big beam. Facing me, she watched without blinking as I stumbled toward her.

I was a couple yards away from her when she finally broke one of her wrists loose. Without hesitation, she bent down and picked up a sharp slab of splintered wood. Like an anchor, the remains of the chair still attached to her other arm, weighed her down to one side.

Wendy raised and pointed the sharp end of debris at me.

I stopped.

The universe will shove you into a corner. You could fight it, leave it, or stay put. I had already tried two of those options, and they didn't work.

"This is how it ends."

With my arms spread like wings, I closed my eyes and charged at Wendy.

The wooden stake pierced my heart and the pain soon faded into numbness.

Wendy's back slammed against the wall as I forced all my body weight against her, sending the stake deeper and deeper into my chest.

She muffled a grunt as the blunt end pushed against hers.

My face was no more than an inch from hers, I opened my eyes and a final rush of euphoria consumed me.

The last thing I saw were her eyes. They reminded me of murky pond on a moonlit night.

My vision faded and I returned to the comfortable void.

OTHER BOOKS BY A.A. MEDINA

DEVIL DANCERS
(WESTERN/FOLK HORROR)

A STORY OF AN UNLIKELY TRIO WHO MUST BAND TOGETHER AND SAVE THE WORLD FROM AN ANCIENT EVIL HELLBENT ON SEVERING THE CONNECTION TO THE SPIRIT OF ALL LIVING THINGS.

WHERE DRAGONFLIES DANCE
(SUPERNATURAL HORROR/MYSTERY)

DRAGGED THROUGH AN EMOTIONAL AND PAINFUL MINEFIELD, A FATHER UNRAVELS THE MYSTERY OF HIS DAUGHTER'S DISAPPEARANCE.

GOD FORBID
(HORROR & SCIENCE FICTION)

A COLLECTION OF ELEVEN SHORT STORIES.

A. A. MEDINA IS AN AUTHOR, EDITOR, GRAPHIC DESIGNER, AND ARTIST BASED OUT OF PHOENIX, ARIZONA. HIS WORK HAS APPEARED IN NUMEROUS PUBLICATIONS. HE WORKS AS A FULL-TIME GRAPHIC DESIGNER UNDER THE BANNER OF FABLED BEAST DESIGN. WHEN NOT WRITING OR DESIGNING, HE PLAYS WAY TOO MUCH MAGIC: THE GATHERING AND DUNGEONS AND DRAGONS WITH HIS WIFE, BROTHERS, AND CHILDHOOD FRIENDS.